Visitors' Book

Visitors' Book

Short stories of their new homeland
by famous authors now living in Ireland

ARROW BOOKS

Arrow Books Limited
17–21 Conway Street, London W1P 5HL

An imprint of the Hutchinson Publishing Group

London Melbourne Sydney Auckland
Johannesburg and agencies
throughout the world

First published by Poolbeg Press 1979

Arrow edition 1982

Made and printed in Great Britain
by The Anchor Press Ltd
Tiptree, Essex

ISBN 0 09 924520 5

Contents

PATRICK SKENE CATLING

The Right Spot

When Kevin J. O'Driscoll, a grizzled but lively blue-eyed ectomorph, retired from his associate professorship of geology at the University of Maryland, he did what he had always wanted to do since the bedtime stories he had been told in his grandmother's lap. He came to live in Ireland.

He brought Birgitta, his wife, with him. She was a good wife, even though she was not of Irish descent. She had good Scandinavian blonde hair, a good, roundish face with pink markings, good conformation and a good way of going. Because she loved him, she left behind the garden club and the supermarkets of College Park, Maryland, without even a murmur of complaint. She felt that she was accompanying Kevin on a pilgrimage, and so she was.

They landed at Shannon one soft summer morning in Year Three of the Age of Inflation, when the American dollar bought only a small part of an Irish pound, which itself was not what it had been. After the excitement of the first aerial glimpse of green through the grey clouds and the pleasure of hearing the gentle voices of the Customs and Immigration inspectors, Kevin was a bit dismayed by the high cost of hiring a small, tinny French car; but of course they could not very easily explore the country without a car. His plastic wallet of traveller's cheques felt thin and his academic pension suddenly seemed precariously meagre.

"Don't worry, Kevin," Birgitta said, smiling bravely and squeezing his arm. "We'll manage. Somehow."

"Of course we will," he agreed, while silently praying to ancestral ghosts that he had not been too grossly misinformed by the Kodachrome enticements of Bord Failte and by a jaunty book he had just read, *So You Want to Live in Ireland,* by the author of *So You Want to Live in Mexico* and *So You Want to Live in Tahiti.*

They drove in a south-westerly direction through landscapes as temperately romantic as Victorian water colours, beneath sunlit scud that diffused rainbows of extravagant promise. Half way around the Ring of Kerry they vowed that they must live forthwith and for ever on the shore of Dingle Bay. However, a brief visit to an estate agent's office in Killarney convinced them that they had arrived several years too late. All the best views in those parts had been taken long before and they were now much too expensive.

Farther south, beyond Kenmare, beyond Glengarriff, even beyond Bantry, they stopped for lunch at a small bar. It was run by an alert publican by the name of Rory Keane, who happened to dabble on the side in property, the undertaking trade and local government. He had a lavishly rubicund complexion and a reliable cable-stitch white jersey. As he removed the sandwich plates, he said:

"I couldn't help overhearing a word or two. It's a house you want, is it? A small class of a private dwelling that would keep the rain off and the wind out. A cosy home where a man could put his feet up and smoke a pipe by the fire in the evening without a worry in the world and his wife could bake a loaf of soda bread and fry the rashers and brew a grand pot of hot tea. A sturdy, well-found building with solid walls and a complete set of roof-slates and a bit of land of its own around it — only enough, not too much. And *reasonable.* Is that it?"

"That's it," Kevin confirmed with a ruefully lopsided smile. "We've been looking for three days. We had no idea the prices would be so high."

"Not all the prices," Keane pointed out, raising a corrective forefinger and smiling reassuringly. "It's only a question of coming to the right man with the right information. This is your lucky day. You have come to him."

"You know of a house for sale?" Kevin asked.

"I do of course. I know of *the* house. Stay away from the strand; that's the secret. Go inland. Do you understand my meaning?"

"We want to live near the sea," Birgitta said.

Keane nodded at her and gave her the sort of smile that a kindergarten teacher might give to a not very bright child that is doing its best. He turned back seriously to Kevin, man to man.

"There's no part of this country far from the sea," Keane said.

"No, I suppose not," Kevin conceded.

"There's no need to do any supposing. I guarantee it. I was born and bred in this country. If you backed away more than seventy miles from any one coast you'd already be approaching nearer than that to another. It's a feature of the geography that you can rely on at all times. It's a first-class arrangement for the sea-lover."

"We want to be able to see the sea," Birgitta said.

"You don't have to get your feet wet to do that," the publican jovially assured her. "There are hills."

After a great deal more talk, Kevin began to experience the fatigue that often induces a sense of fatalism in West Cork late in the afternoon. When Keane called his wife to take over the bar and urged the O'Driscolls to get into their car to follow him, Kevin acceded.

They took a side road off the coast road and a back road off the side road and turned into a steep, narrow, tortuous track of loose stones between blackberry bushes and bracken and then through a wooden gateway and along a rutted path between boulders and gorse bushes and startled rabbits and came at last to a cottage of classic West Cork design, with none of the right-angles too pedantically exact, and with two chimneys, one at each end, and a fresh coat of whitewash.

"This is a typical upland limestone river valley between parallel foldings of Old Red Sandstone," Kevin observed.

Keane did not wish to commit himself on that aspect of the property, so, for a moment, he remained silent.

"What about electricity?" Birgitta asked, having noticed no external wires.

He was up to questions of that sort and indeed on top of them entirely.

"The E.S.B. can make all the necessary arrangements for the electricity," he promised her. "I can put you in touch personally with the man in Bantry who understands the whole procedure backwards. He's a regular customer of mine. It would be a matter of a telephone call."

"Of course the house has no telephone."

"That could be installed after you have the electricity," he patiently told her. Dear God! American women! "You would have to submit an application to the proper authorities. There is a form. It isn't difficult to fill in. I'll tell you what: while you're waiting for your own telephone you can use mine. There's a grand telephone for telephoning from right in the bar."

"Ireland is a very interesting example of glacial drift,"

Kevin said.

Birgitta was too tired for geology, even in its most dramatic manifestations.

"And water?" she asked.

"Water?" Keane exclaimed. "The water is gorgeous. There's no better water anywhere else at all in the thirty-two counties. Sixty inches of it every year, without fail."

"I only asked," she said rather apologetically, "because I read in the paper the other day that they were considering rationing water in Dublin."

"Dublin is Dublin," he explained.

Keane sensed a danger that the woman might start asking a lot more questions about petty technicalities, if he let her. It was time for the bold approach. He told them the price. He, himself, had sold the same property for five hundred pounds only ten years ago; the new price was four thousand per cent more; but the O'Driscolls were not to know that; they would not comprehend the intricacies of the expanding Irish economy. It would have been a shame to confuse them. As things were, they were pleasantly surprised to learn that the house cost slightly less than the split-level California-style ranchhouse they had recently sold in College Park.

That night they stayed above the bar, which was also a garage, a grocery and a guesthouse. In bed, they talked until long after midnight about the prices of houses around Killarney and the price of the house they had just seen. They agreed that they were not really taking advantage of someone who did not know what he was doing, and the very next morning after breakfast, before anyone could change his mind, they clinched the deal.

For Kevin and Birgitta it was a happy summer, almost like a second honeymoon. The long, slow days were golden with unexpected sunshine. They worked together, steadily improving their cottage, without straining themselves. They discovered the soothing fragrance and the mild stimulation of tea, the comfort of the tea break. They adjusted to the calm tick of Cork Time. The fresh, mild Atlantic air of summer was conducive to cheerful conciliation and serene acceptance, to many daytime postponements without guilt or rancour and to nights of blissfully profound sleep.

"I bet bees make delicious honey from all this heather around here," Kevin said one drowsy warm morning.

"Mmm," Birgitta agreed.

"I think I'll get a few beehives. We'd have our own bee-loud glade. The bees would do the work. All you'd have to do would be to help yourself to the honey."

"Yeats," she murmured, as though unreproachfully catching him pilfering. "I saw the library book. Since when have you been a reader of poetry?"

"Maybe I'll build the hives myself," he said.

"When are you going to start?"

"I don't know. Soon, I expect."

"Will you get up if I make the tea?"

"Soon," he repeated, smiling and reaching for her.

In their second-hand Mini, Birgitta sometimes drove to nearby towns — Skibbereen, Dunmanway, Clonakilty and Bandon, to mention but a few — to look for antique farmhouse furniture. She made these casual, leisurely expeditions in the name of practicality and economy, though really the pleasure of the search was usually an end in itself. Even so, she did find an old kitchen dresser and a massive kitchen table, which a local butcher kindly picked up and delivered in his lorry. When she had painstakingly stripped the paint off these pieces of furniture and varnished them, they became more precious to her than anything by Chippendale or Sheraton could have been.

Kevin gained the friendship of a fisherman with one eye and an orange beard like a leprechaun's ambush. He was known as Terry The Hook. The name was said to have something to do with his empty socket. He looked like a pirate but he would not have hurt a winkle, except, of course, by eating it. After lengthy strategic conferences at Keane's, Terry occasionally took Kevin out in the bay in a rowing boat with an outboard motor. When the mackerel were running in great abundance late in August, Kevin caught more of them than anyone in his right mind could actually have wanted.

"We're so lucky," Birgitta said.

"I know," he replied.

Early one evening, at the calm time of the sunset, as Terry was tying up at the quay, Kevin noticed that the pink blossoms of the thrift on the grey sea wall were drooping and withered. Their premature decline was a disturbing omen. It was not the only one. There were tourists with red sunburn. Farmers shook their heads and spoke of drought.

As the water from their taps flowed in diminishing trickles, the O'Driscolls studied the meteorological synoptic charts in *The Cork Examiner* and listened to the RTE weather forecasts with increasing concern. There was a procession of *H*'s across the Atlantic to West Cork of a continuity unprecedented since records were first kept; the *L*'s all passed northwards: Iceland must have been experiencing rainfall worthy of *The Guinness Book of Records.*

The O'Driscolls' water supply came to them in the simplest way, by gravity, through a rubber pipe like a long garden hose whose upper end was immersed in a stream embedded in a limestone channel about fifty yards above the house. There were no other houses and no pasture between the O'Driscolls and the top of the hill and the water seemed pure. Certainly it had not been recycled several times through innumerable human bodies and chemically treated like the water distributed in some large cities.

"No wonder the pressure's down," Kevin said after an anxious inspection. "The stream's only two or three inches deep." In June its depth had been about two feet.

"I wonder what we should do," he said.

"You're the scientist," his wife reminded him.

"Yes," he acknowledged doubtfully. "I suppose what we really need is a well. And that would mean the noise of a pump."

They had become accustomed to profound silences, interrupted by only the wind, the cries of seagulls, the barks of faraway dogs and other natural country sounds.

"And God knows what it would cost. That would depend largely on how far down we had to go."

"Geology," Birgitta said.

"In this respect, it's only a science of probabilities. There's always an element of chance."

"We must have water," she said.

Keane said he had a friend in the well-drilling business; the drilling of a well would be easy to arrange.

"The question is: where?" Kevin said fretfully, thinking aloud. "I can't afford to make a mistake."

"Good man!" Keane said. "You're right. That's the question. You've got to pick the right spot. That's why you need a dowser. Before you start the drilling, a dowser's your only man. I have a friend . . ."

Kevin was sceptical. He did not believe in divination by crystal ball, tea-leaves, chicken entrails or even the disposition of the stars at the place and moment of one's birth, though Birgitta insisted upon reading their daily astrological forecasts in the paper just to be on the safe side. Could anyone really detect underground water with a hazel wand?

"Paddy can," Keane said. "He can if anyone can," he added more exactly. "It's a knack. He's found a terrible number of places for well-boring in these parts."

Kevin refrained from saying that it would be possible to hit water just about anywhere below the surface of West Cork. Anyway, Paddy's charge for the job was modest. Kevin asked him to try.

Paddy bicycled over the next afternoon. He was a small, dark, furtive man with a beaky inquisitive nose and cunning eyes. He looked as though he were searching for something that might be hard to find. After a glass of whisky, he gave the O'Driscolls a confident smile.

"Now," he said.

Kevin accompanied him as he walked to and fro, as slowly and steadily as a sleep-walker, across the acre of rocks and gorse, his two hands at arms' length in front of him, holding the double end of the Y-shaped wand, with the single end straight ahead and parallel with the ground.

Suddenly Paddy seemed to awaken: his whole body became tense; his nose twitched excitedly; his hands trembled and shook, and the wand pointed almost straight down. He turned toward Kevin triumphantly as though he had told him so.

"There you are," Paddy said.

To Kevin, as a geologist, that particular spot seemed as suitable as any other.

When Keane's friend the well-digger drove around a couple of days later with a rotary drilling rig, Kevin showed him the chosen site. He did not take very long to get started.

The roaring of the motor and the grinding of the bit down through the rock went on and on, all morning and all afternoon.

"Not yet," said the well-digger, having switched off. He smiled encouragingly. "But it could be any time now. I'll carry on first thing tomorrow."

The drilling continued for several hours the following day. Kevin kept asking about the depth of the shaft and calculating the cost. He was sitting at the kitchen table, sipping tea and trying to appear to be calm, when the sound of the motor stopped. After a few moments there was a timid knock at the kitchen door.

"I'm sorry, Mr. O'Driscoll," the man said. "But you've had some bad luck. We'll have to drill somewhere else. It's filthy, the stuff down there; it isn't fit to drink."

Most petroleum deposits are found between twenty-five thousand and five hundred feet below the surface; however, upward seepage occasionally occurs, through vertical fractures and fissures in the rock. This was one of those occasions. Kevin immediately observed that they had struck oil. He did not say so. He only said:

"Of course what we have here is a sedimentary basin."

"Don't worry," the well-digger said. "There's plenty of good water. Maybe we should drill farther down the slope. Would you like me to try that?"

"Not now," Kevin said. "I think you'd better take the rig away for the time being at least. I'll let you know if I need it again."

The well-digger was very sympathetic.

A little later, Kevin went out alone. Birgitta decided not to ask him what was on his mind. He walked down to Keane's. It was a beautiful walk: the hills across the bay were gilded by the light of the setting sun; the water was amber and oyster-grey. He saw Terry's boat coming in from a day's fishing.

Kevin knew he should order a bottle of champagne, but he didn't really feel like celebrating. He doubted that there was a bottle of champagne in the house — Keane preferred to keep things simple — and Kevin liked it that way. He got a pint of Guinness at the bar and sat quietly by himself in a corner and stared thoughtfully into the future.

He saw a big new house, big cars and a big cabin cruiser moored beside a new private quay. He saw a forest of oil derricks all over the hillside and wide new roads and rows of bungalows, a company town. He saw a refinery and factories and more houses and a shopping centre. He saw administrators, engineers, technicians and mechanics. He saw Keane's Select Bar enormously enlarged and improved beyond recognition, with fluorescent lighting and wall-to-wall carpet and chrome and plastic all over the place and a juke box and one-armed bandits, the big room crowded with strangers shouting in strange languages. He shook his head to clear it and resolutely clenched his right fist.

"Are you all right?" Birgitta asked solicitously when he got home.

"Yes," he said. "I'm fine."

"I was worried."

"Don't worry. You can't expect water diviners and well-diggers to be infallible. I'll go up to the stream with buckets. And if that runs dry I'll take the buckets somewhere else — Skibbereen if necessary! Cork! Limerick! Anywhere. We'll be all right."

"I'm glad that's the way you feel," she said, smiling. "When you went down to Keane's I looked at the place where the man had been drilling."

"Hopeless, I'm afraid. Quite undrinkable."

"Quite," she agreed. "And I've never wanted an oilwell either."

That evening the RTE forecaster predicted showers followed by heavy rain, and he was right.

MALCOLM MACDONALD

The Last Holiday in Ireland

It must have been the explosion that threw him out the top bunk. Yet he came awake a split second before he hit the deck, and he heard the bang just an instant later. At such moments our senses offer all kinds of contradictions.

The ship began to list almost at once.

"Torpedo." The word punctuated half a dozen frantic conversations in the corridor outside. His mother said it, too: "We must have been hit by a torpedo." But she was almost nonchalant.

"Can we go to our lifeboat?" Mark asked.

"Better get dressed," she said. "And put on your lifejackets."

"But what about the lifeboat?" asked Alex, Mark's younger brother.

"Put on your fur coats under your lifejackets," she added.

There had been no official lifeboat drill since they had sailed from Greenock, five days before, but Mark and Alex, despairing of a lead from the Merchant Navy, had spent one of those days doing some private-enterprise running and mustering with some of the other children. The grown-ups had smiled tolerantly.

"Where *is* our lifeboat?" their mother asked, as if she doubted they even had one.

"On the afterdeck on the port side," Mark said.

At the same time Alex said, "Lifeboat station B. All the cabins on this corridor are the same."

They both spoke with impatient scorn, for the plan showing every lifeboat station was displayed in all the corridors and cabins.

"Well boys, don't be afraid," she said. "I'm sure we're going to be all right."

It hadn't occurred to either boy to be afraid. This was a new adventure in a war that — though barely two years old — had already offered a surfeit of adventures: bombs and other loud noises in the night, dead German pilots stretched in their sodden sheepskins on the beach, wrecked Heinkels that smelled of a very unBritish sort of bakelite, a night-time countryside darker than even cavemen had known it, walls with ears, spies in every hedge . . . and now torpedoes.

Moons of Galway. That's where they'd bought the lovely,

warm fur coats, at the end of that last holiday in Ireland, the last holiday before the war. They had to beat Germany now before they could go back to Ireland; if they went back before Germany was beaten, the Irish would intern them. Mark still wasn't sure what that meant, but it sounded like being turned inside out.

Their mother cast a last glance around the cabin; but her two sons, anxious to be off on the new adventure, tugged at her hands.

"Gloves," she said.

Grumpily Alex fished his gloves out of the footlocker. The lights dimmed, brightened . . . dimmed, and went out. Only then did they realise how silent the ship had been since the torpedo. In the dark of the corridor, a voice said, "Does anyone know where we muster?" It was the father of the stuck-up girl, Veronica. Mark called her stuck-up; secretly he called her beautiful, too. Months later he had splendid daydreams of this moment: a wall of water leaping at them down the corridor, and himself clutching Veronica in his strong, lithe arms and battling her through the maelstrom to safety. "Two survivors . . . ." the bulletins all said. They wept for their dead families and hugged each other deliciously.

But that was all later. On the night itself he did not think of Veronica at all, not even when her father spoke.

Their mother said, "Life Station B. Abaft the port side." And though she got it wrong, she spoke with such immense assurance (her customary public tone) that even Mark and Alex found themselves half-believing her version more than their, official, one.

A dull thud that swiftly became resonant welcomed them on deck. Then another. Then another. There was a flash out to sea, about a quarter of a mile away.

"Right! That does it," a seaman said. "Come on lads."

In the bright moonlight Mark watched them swarm up the sides of the after deckhouse and throw the covers off the gun. *The* gun, the ship's one and only. It glistened with greasy highlights. An officer shinned up after them. "Good show," he said.

"Two inch," Alex said confidently. "Or even three."

There was something hot in Mark's shoe; he danced and

bent to wriggle it out with his fingers. It looked like a bit of coke with two sides polished smooth; but it was much heavier than coke. And it was almost too hot to handle. "Look," he said. "Shrapnel. They must be shelling us."

Four seamen were struggling to get the port-side lifeboat outboard but the listing of the ship had wedged it on one of the davits. One of them heard Mark. "S'all right, son," he said. "They're all falling up forr'ard. We're safe here."

"Fire!" shouted the gunnery officer.

The air shimmered and rang with the loudest, sharpest, report Mark had ever heard. The sweet, acrid stench of cordite wafted through them. There was a splash far out to starboard, then another, beyond it.

"Ducks-and-drakes!" Mark laughed. "The shell did ducks-and-drakes."

Their father had done twenty ducks-and-drakes with a flat pebble in Errislannen harbour that last holiday in Ireland.

"Look!" Alex said excitedly. "Out to starboard."

Mark followed his pointing finger and saw, on the oily black of the ocean, between them and the now pale oval of the first splash, the slightly less black shape of the submarine.

"If she torpedoed us from starboard, why are we listing to port?" Alex asked. No one answered.

"She won't go no lower, sir," one of the gunners said. "Try her at that?"

"Very well," the officer said. He raised his hand. They heard him draw breath. They waited for his shout of "Fire!" But instead there was an immensely deep, brief whir in the air above them, a crack from the direction of the sub, and, almost instantaneously, a white-plumed splash far out to port. The headless body of the gunnery officer fell among them — "one of the ballistic flukes of the war," a reporter wrote later. The officer's blood was almost as hot as the shrapnel. Mark wiped it off his shoes with his hands and then, surreptitiously, leaning into the darkest dark, he tasted it. His heart hammered frantically at the sin; it tasted like warm, sea-watery gum arabic.

"Why are we listing to port?" Alex repeated.

A breathless officer ran among them. "What bloody fool is firing that gun?" he shouted.

The crowd parted to show him the corpse. "Come down

and get these boats launched," he told the gunners in a gentler voice.

"And Mr. McFarlane, sir?" a seaman asked.

The officer was already going. "Leave him," he called. "There's twenty or more dead below."

"Ahoy!" A Tannoy-magnified voice rolled at them over the water. "City of Nagpur!"

It was so British and so naval in tone that an incredulous cheer arose from the stricken ship. But it went on: "We give you thirty minutes to abandon ship. No shooting. Then we sink you. You may put on your decklights. No more shooting."

"Why are we listing to port if the sub's to starboard?" Alex asked one of the seamen.

"No flies on them," the man said. "Put a torpedo in one side, wait for the list, then surface on the other side. Guns can't train down on them, see?"

"How long before we sink?" Mark asked.

"Long time yet. You'll see some fireworks when we get away. Come on now — last trip round the lighthouse!"

Grown-ups went down a ropeladder that hung out into space. Children went down three at a time in a sack. It was a slow way to get fifty people into a lifeboat, but its very tedium banished all sense of panic. Some even flopped, with self-conscious weariness, onto the deck as they waited their turn.

The seas had appeared almost calm from the ship, but in the small boat the swell was alarming, especially in the dark. The flickering moonlight defined only the ripples, leaving the larger waves unmarked; they ambushed the lifeboat, hoisting her in surprise and letting her lurch back into signless voids, sometimes long, sometimes short, but never with any predictable rhythm.

By the time the half-hour truce was up, all the lifeboats were well clear of the abandoned ship. With her lights blazing and the smoke curling from her funnels she looked more like a haven than a death trap. But then the promised "fireworks" began: fifty-three shells and two further torpedoes, spread over twenty raucous minutes.

"A gallant little ship!" Veronica's father said. He was a

BBC man going out to All India Radio.

"That's a captured French sub," one of the sailors said. "They're using the old Nagpur as familiarisation."

At last the ship turned on her side, sank by the bow, vanished, reappeared, briefly poking twenty foot of her stern up through the heart of a boiling white sea, then disappeared for good.

"She's still got her lights on," Mark said.

There was a deep rumble, somewhere below the water.

"One boiler gone. Two to go," the sailor told them.

Suddenly Mark stood up in panic. "Teddy!" he cried. He'd left his Teddy behind — poor one-eyed Ted, deprived of half his sight and most of his fur by a love both long and intense.

"You can't do anything about it now," their mother told him.

"Teddy! Teddy!" Mark wailed.

"Grow up!" Alex said, embarrassed.

The sailor on the bench in front turned round and hugged Mark as well as their lifejackets allowed. "'Tis an honour to go down with a ship," he said. "And when we're rescued, you'll see, we'll do the proper thing by him."

Alex wanted to ask what was "the proper thing." But to Mark the enormous vagueness of the promise was its attraction. He was reconciled at once to the loss. "It wasn't only Teddy," he explained. "I forgot all my emergency rations, too."

It had taken days to assemble and pack them in a Mr. Barrett's shoebox: a bag of lentils, fishooks and line, aspirin, a bottle of fresh water . . . even a half bar of precious, precious chocolate.

Tat-tat-tat-tat . . . the noise was chillingly familiar from the newsreels.

"Down!" The cry came from another lifeboat. "Heads down."

But heads were already down. They all knew the sound of machinegun fire. The little wasp noises overhead were unexpected, though.

"Sorry about that." The navy-like voice rolled over the waters to the stupefied boats. "Orders. I hope we didn't actually hit anyone — we aimed well over your heads. We can spare you another half hour. If you have any wounded, we have a doctor and medicines aboard, so show a light."

A signalling lamp began to flash half a mile away. With the aid of its searchlight the sub threaded its way among them to the source of the signal.

"Bastards!" the sailor said.

"Here, watch your language!" their mother told him.

"Hear, hear," Veronica's father said.

All that night the lifeboats called and signalled to one another so that by dawn they formed a long, drifting chain, each boat a rope's length apart. The third and last boiler exploded about four a.m.—three hours after the sinking. The detonation reaching up from the seabed, seemed to stretch the skin of the ocean. Everyone was seasick. But they were all cheered up by the news that the Sparks had spent twenty minutes broadcasting an S.O.S. and their position.

"They'd hear that round the world, so they would," the sailor said. His name, they learned, was Tiger Reilly. The boys thought Tiger the most wonderful Christian name ever. When they were seasick, he wet his fingers with brandy and wiped it on their lips; for years afterward the very smell of brandy made their stomachs queasy.

An hour after dawn a Catalina flying boat spotted them. "The Navy is sinking the Graf Spee, just down the road," it signalled. Veronica's father, and several sailors, spelled out the flashing letters; another sailor wrote them down. Half the lifeboat called out the words in laughing excitement until the other half quelled them with cries of *Shhh*! in case the scribe should miss, or mishear, a letter.

Apparently a destroyer, returning from the Graf Spee operation, would be rerouted to rescue them. Apparently, too, there was a lifeboat full of lascars two miles to their south. Until then no one had realised that the lascars, the dogsbodies of the City of Nagpur, were rather thinly represented in the ranks of the survivors.

The captain ordered one of the lifeboats to distribute its civilians among the others and row off in search of the lascars.

"Waste of time and men," Tiger muttered.

"Some of your shipmates may be among them," their mother said.

Mark wondered what a lascar looked like; he hadn't noticed them on the ship.

When the lifeboat had gone on the captain's errand, the day settled into a routine that made any one hour exactly like the rest. The swell was mountainous — a succession of broad, rolling hills of water. From afar each crest seemed full of menace, certain to swamp the tiny string of boats, each with its fifty-odd passengers. But the incline was so long and gradual that the upward lilt was quite gentle; indeed, it seemed that every wave flattened as it passed under them. Only from the tops could they see the horizon — and only from the tops of the higher waves, at that.

At about three o'clock that afternoon, after the second ration of biscuits and water, a new phenomenon appeared among them: hallucination. "Surely it's high time the destroyer found us . . . ." It was said a hundred times in each of the lifeboats. That expectation, together with their tiredness, led to countless spurious — though passionately sincere — sightings of smoke or masts on distant horizons.

"Here's a big one," people said, watching a vast, grey-green wall of ocean bear down on them. "Ho-oo-oop!" they laughed as the tiny craft skittered up its side. But at the top a rapt silence fell while they scanned the farthest skylines, where anything — a freak upward cusp of wave, some windblown spume, a spar floating a mere furlong away — *anything,* could be conjured into a "There she is!"

"Where? Where?"

"There!"

But too late. The boat would already be plummeting down into the blue-black valley beyond. And then it might be several minutes before another wave would lift them high enough to check the sighting. Always it turned out to be false.

No one was immune — from the most seasoned sailor to the merest infant, all saw, all knew beyond doubt they had seen, the rescue ship. Long after they stopped shouting out their discoveries they went on seeing her.

At four o'clock their own rescue boat returned with the lascars — about two hundred of them, crowded into the two boats. "How they survived in one for the best part of twelve hours, God alone knows," the sailors said. The lascars were shared out equally among the other boats — about thirty more souls apiece. Suddenly they were much more crowded. Everyone grumbled.

Mark was disappointed by the lascars; they were just people. Skinny, brown men, huddling together and chattering with fright. No one else was frightened — or, at least, no one else showed any fear. That, more than the colour of their skins, marked these new arrivals off from the rest. Mark resented them for their fear; it was a note that had been absent from this marvellous adventure until now.

"We've got to lighten ship," the officer said. With the lascars they had acquired an officer, too. "You two boys had better put those fur coats overboard."

"But why?" asked their astounded mother.

"If they went into the water with those, they'd sink," he told her.

"Despite their lifejackets?"

He remembered his rank. "Jettison them," he ordered.

They took off their coats and dropped them overboard. Their mother did not complain. War was war.

There was a calm in the lee of the boat. The fur coats took a long time to sink. They made a rust-coloured patch, astonishing in the grey-green of the water. All the warmth in the world seemed to be sinking with them. *I could still reach down and get it back,* he thought. Then, *I could still dive down* . . . . Then, *If Daddy was here, he could dive down.* . . .

The waters swallowed the last, faintest blush of the coats. From Moons of Galway, just before the war. He lifted his eyes to the sky . . . and to a new wonder: Errislannan!

"Look," he said excitedly to Alex." There's Clifden. And the white madonna! And the doctor's . . . look, even the lake! And Mrs. Joyce's! And Jellyfish Bay!"

"And the coral beach . . . and Errislannen harbour!" Alex saw it as clearly as his brother.

For a moment they were both silent in wonder. The recreation in the clouds was so perfect — even the beach where the man had drowned, though neither felt able to point it out. Not here.

"Look, Mummy!" they said excitedly.

"Pure imagination," she said, not really looking at the

clouds.

"'Tis a grand gift," Tiger Reilly told her.

She smiled. "I can hear you're from Ireland, Mr. Reilly," she said. "D'you know that part of Connemara? We were there in the summer of thirty-nine."

"God, I don't. I'm from Dublin," Reilly said as if it were a complete justification for his ignorance of Connemara.

"But that's not far, is it, Tiger?" Alex assured him. (Alex who had fretted through the eternal five hours of car journey which separated the two coasts of Ireland!)

"No," Tiger Reilly agreed. "No more than three centuries, I'd say."

"We can't go back to Ireland," Alex said. "Not until we've won the war."

"Or the Irish will intern us," Mark explained.

"Sure we wouldn't," Tiger Reilly said. "Whoever told ye such a tale!"

His laugh was cut short by a violent rocking of the boat.

While Mark had rediscovered the Errislannen peninsula in the sky, several of the crew had been putting up the awning at the stern of the lifeboat — a light affair of spars and canvas. They had intended it for the women and children in case they weren't rescued before nightfall; but the lascars, shivering in their thin cotton clothing, made one concerted rush for it as soon as the work was complete. They vanished into its dark womb, still chattering their alien fear. Only their eyes and teeth gleamed dully in the gloom.

Tiger Reilly half rose and pulled his oilskin coat out from under him. He hitched it up behind and held it with his left hand. His right furled up the hem of his rollneck sweater to reveal a large knife in a worn leather scabbard. A practised dig of his thumbnail flipped open the clasp. The knife was half withdrawn when a hand — their mother's — reached between the two fascinated boys.

"No," she said.

Reilly looked round. "It's them or us, so it is," he answered.

"Not now," she said. "Think of the children. Wait until dark at least."

Reluctantly Reilly agreed; he thrust the knife back into its scabbard and let his oilskin fall.

Never before had Mark been so close to hitting his mother. He hated her with an intensity that shocked him. If Tiger killed the lascars now, he'd be able to watch. But she'd gone and spoiled it. After dark he'd see nothing. Damn her! Damn her!

"What're you going to do, Tiger?" he asked, hoping by his excitement to show he didn't mind, hoping to rekindle the man's resolve.

"Ah . . . just threaten them," Tiger said easily.

"Knife them," Mark said.

Tiger laughed.

"Knife them and throw them overboard."

The laughter redoubled. "As you say, ma'am. A great imagination they have!"

In eighteen hours adrift, Mark learned more of himself and of mankind than was entirely good for a nine-year-old. But it was still a very little learning. And Nature, who discovered the dangers of a little learning long before Alexander Pope, soon turned his eyes skyward, among the clouds, searching again for Connemara and the locus of that last marvellous holiday before the war.

Nothing was left. Harbour, lake, beaches . . . the doctor's house . . . Mrs. Joyce's . . . all were gone, replaced by an unknown nowhere of a coastline in the sky. Not even a coastline. Just . . . clouds.

The loss of that glimpse of Connemara was the greatest of all these losses he suffered since the first torpedo had catapulted him from his bunk.

The rescue destroyer came within half a mile before anyone dared to shout, "There she is!"

JOHN ARDEN

The Fork in the Head

Jackson came back to Galway after two weeks in London 'meeting potential clients' — he had not met very many, and had wasted most of his afternoons in the cinema watching insipid films about naked women: but he had succeeded in conducting *some* business, and was able to inform Fionnuala that although progress was rather slow it was nonetheless "appreciable". She looked at him sideways and said, "See any good movies?"

"Oh yes — one, anyway — Japanese. Very sadistic, Samurai: but offbeat. I'd had lunch with Jack Levison, and hadn't anyone else to see that day — Macgregor had cried off. The Academy in Oxford Street. How did you spend your time?" Fionnuala grinned at him, ubiquitous, omniscient: certainly maddeningly superior. "How do you suppose? There was a meeting in Eyre Square about the Republican Prisoners and I made a speech. O'Reilly and his crowd tried to exclude me from the platform but Maeve Hanratty and the Red Tendency Group insisted that it was a united front or nothing and in the end I had to be accepted. But they wouldn't let me march immediately behind the banner, and Maeve and I ended up at the end of the demo amongst the odds and sods. What's your opinion?"

"Eh . . . ? Oh, well, so long as you actually were on the march and you did get to say your bit, I suppose it was okay?"

"It was bloody hell *not* okay, Jackson. There is a definite attempt to manoeuvre the whole Group out of the campaign. What are you going to do about it?"

Jackson did not want to do anything about it. His lady's political alliances, confederations, and country-dance permutations were so fluid and progressive as to be always one move beyond his immediate comprehension. Besides, while he had been in London there had been a tolerably large Irish meeting at Kilburn about the Prisoners, which Fionnuala would have wished him to attend, which he knew he ought to have attended, and from which he had been inexcusably absent — he had in fact been at the Cinecenta off Leicester Square between two-thirty and six, sprawled in front of something French called "Midnight Streets" . . . or had it been "Women of the Night Streets" . . . ? Anyway, he had the uneasy feeling that Fionnuala must have read about the

Kilburn meeting in one or other of the her mail-order news sheets, Republican or Trotskyite, and she would certainly ask him for an account of it. He changed the subject and went into the kitchen to make some more coffee. When he came back into the studio, Fionnuala had his portfolio open, and was prowling through the various drawings he had or had not managed to sell in London, and the conversation became mercifully professional.

Jackson was a 'layout designer' and Fionnuala had been a children's book illustrator. He had originally met her when he was on a visit to Dublin to attend an exhibition of Irish posters and book-jackets. After a year or two's random contact, in and out of Ireland, in and out of bed, and in and out of various emotional absurdities, they had settled down together to produce freelance 'visual motifs'. His alleged business acumen kept them together as a 'firm', while her creative talent was responsible for the actual work. They had gone to live in Galway, where a series of state and semi-state subsidies were always about to come through as a result of drinks bought in lounge bars for enthusiastic but unreliable local politicians. There was some notion of their setting up a weekend school for young graduate designers in connection with UCG. Fionnuala — in Jackson's opinion — did not improve the chances of this project by taking part in so much national-liberationism. Jackson — in Fionnuala's opinion — did not improve the creative quality of their joint work by refusing to recognise his political backwardness.

Their relationship, already under stress from his Britishness and her Irishness, had lately become exceedingly unstable — or so at least it might have seemed to their intimates. But then intimates are rarely as intimate as all that: and in fact the pair of them managed remarkably well. Probably the real reason they still held together was that he loved her drawings; and she loved the way he could adapt and develop her drawings within the context of the industries they served. At all events, they had not seriously quarrelled over anything for very long. Despite her political obsessions — as he regarded it — she was a decent, tolerant, and courageous person; and despite his laziness and egocentricity — as she regarded it — he had never questioned the correctness of the left-republican line on the national issue — and he was a very good cook.

Sexually they were perhaps but moderately compatible. But there is a certain sensuality to be derived from the joint production of even plastic carrier-bag designs: and there is no doubt that they took full advantage of this.

The day after his return from his London fortnight, Jackson said they ought to be going to the island for the good weather. This island was in the middle of the big lake, and had on it one small weatherboarded fishing-cabin. When they had no engagements, but needed peace and quiet to develop a new line of work, they would get into their Volkswagen, drive into the Galway shopping centre, fill up the back of the car with boxes of tinned food and bottles of wine, and then drive about ten miles to the small strand where they kept their boat. Jackson would start to fool about with the outboard motor, while Fionnuala went behind a hedge to urinate. When she had finished, he would abandon the useless motor, and they would row out across to the island, a distance of about half a mile. They would unlock the cabin, collect twigs and dead branches, light a fire on the hearth, cook some sausages, and boil a kettle for coffee or tea. Jackson would eat the sausages. Fionnuala would gather blackberries from the brambles all round the back of the cabin and eat them. She thought that sausages were conducive to fat and eventual cardiac trouble. He thought that the island blackberries were full of worms. It would take them the rest of the day to clean up the cabin and assure themselves that the rats had not damaged their things since the last visit. Usually there was a good deal of nasty rat dung everywhere, and a sour smell. They would lay out poison in little tin can lids under the house, which was supported upon six concrete bollards.

Upon this particular occasion, Fionnuala suddenly remembered something. "Oh God," she said, just as Jackson put his last piece of sausage into his mouth. "I have suddenly remembered something." It appeared that there was to be another demo, or march, or picket, or whatever, in Galway, the following evening: and she had suddenly remembered it. It was all Jackson's bloody fault she had forgotten it, going on so much about his damned Japanese films. She had promised Maeve that she would be at the Tavern at two o'clock for a preliminary laying-of-plans.

"Let Maeve get up her own riots on her own for a change, for God's sake," said Jackson. "If the freedom of Ireland cannot proceed without your personal presence at every damned meeting, then all I can say is that the Irish people at large are not worthy of such liberty. Ha!" Fionnuala replied that Maeve needed all her friends to counteract O'Reilly and his fucking crowd, and that Jackson ought to be there too, by rights. Jackson said that all they were fucking doing was helping to make fucking O'Reilly into the future Irish Hitler; and he would be buggered if he would do anything to give that sodding hooligan any chance at all to make himself more conspicuous. "To counteract O'Reilly is exactly what he wants," he yelled. "He's bloody using you to advance himself, and in my small opinion he's an agent of the Special Branch!" Fionnuala said that of course O'Reilly was an agent of the Branch: so they had to counteract him. He was ultra-left and infantile: but it had to be recognised that much of what he propounded was nonetheless correct, and therein lay his danger. "The student element will always go for the O'Reilly line unless someone can expose it. You ought to be in there, Jackson, doing your utmost. You're well enough known, for God's sake, and the young people respect you."

"Do they fuck! A bloody Englishman, a blow-in, respect hell. God dammit, Fionnuala, I have made myself a monkey far too long in front of those riff-raff students of yours. I am not going to get involved." And that was that. He rowed her over to the mainland the following morning, saw her off from the strand in the VW, and then returned to the island in great annoyance and paradoxical relief of mind. He made himself a lunch from the last of the sausages, had a glass or two more red wine than he ought to have drunk at that time of a hot day, and stretched himself out on the grass with a large picture-book of erotic Indian miniatures and his transistor radio. He fell asleep. At about four o'clock he woke up, sweating, a little headachy, and bitten all over by the island's hot weather insects. He decided to go out in the boat. He took another bottle of wine and a plastic container of some sort of salad compilation which Fionnuala had bought the previous day at Roche's Stores. He stuck a fork in his hip pocket to eat the salad with, and nearly forgot the corkscrew. He left the Indian miniatures behind in the cabin, and brought, instead, the Penguin translation of Petronius's *Satyricon*. He was going to have a thoroughly self-indulgent afternoon.

He rowed out to the northeast, until the boat was floating easily between two round uninhabited islands where sheep moaned crossly across the water at each other. He pulled in his oars, pushed a cushion into the bows of the boat, and lay down in the sunshine with his book and his wine and his salad. There were no insects out on the lake, thank God. Three-quarters of a mile away were a couple of boats with fishing parties in them. The sky was blue and untroubled. He forked away at his salad, dropping bits of it on the flies of his trousers and the pages of his book. This was a nuisance, so he altered his position, put the book on the thwart, and sat properly to finish his snack. He pulled the wine bottle to his mouth — he had forgotten to bring a cup or glass — and swallowed a large quantity. He felt suddenly surprisingly drunk. He spoke aloud to himself: "I suppose she'll stay in town overnight with that silly Maeve. If she gets in amongst that Lesbian lot, God knows where she'll end up. I don't fucking care. Let her march with O'Reilly or against O'Reilly, on behalf of or in the face of or up the fundament of the bloody Branch. Jackson is drinking his wine."

He was vaguely aware of a series of quick ripples running towards him across the flat lake. He balanced his bottle on the thwart and balanced his salad box on the gunwale and stooped to pick up the fork which had fallen to the bottom boards of the boat. He held the salad box in his left hand and executed an over-large manoeuvre with the fork to pierce a piece of pimento. The ripples and the small squall which moved them surged up to the boat. There was a swift heave of the water, a sudden sway of the boat, the sun went in behind a grey cloud; and the fork fell into the lake. For two long slow seconds he looked down and watched it sink, deep deep and glistering like a dream of a fish into the dark green water and the aspiring darkness of the water weeds. Then all of a hurry, he dumped the salad box back inboard, saved the wine bottle, which was rolling off the thwart, grabbed hold of his oars and thrust them onto the rowlocks, and began to row back to the island.

It had become chilly and he had not bothered to bring his shirt. The wind rose as he pulled across the water, and his bare skin shuddered. A few small spikes of rain pricked on to his shoulders. The pages of his book were all spotted with wet brownish circles as it lay, open, in the bottom of the boat. When he landed he discovered that his cushion was quite damp. He did not bother to take it with him as he went up to the cabin and made himself a pot of tea.

That evening the wind continued to rise, blowing from the west, from the mainland onto the island. The rain rattled on the corrugated iron roof of the cabin with an undue amount of noise, as though a shower bath had been inadvertently left on. This cabin, being roofed with metal and walled with a double layer of light plank, had all the properties of a sounding-box — in rough weather it was like living inside a banjo. He listened to the radio as he lay on his bunk and smoked cigarettes. There was a lengthy programme of Irish and English folk song, introduced by a very solemn commentator who talked heavily about ethnic values for five minutes between every two minute musical item. Jackson enjoyed folk music and even sang it — when there was no one to hear him. He could not indicate the difference between one note and the other, which made it impossible for him to perform for other people's musical pleasure. But he was good at delivering the meaning of the words and could even suggest a certain poetical passion in his renditions. It had been his ability to do this which had originally got him into Fionnuala's bed — or so he believed. He could in fact sing himself into a state of amorous excitement. He ignored the pedantic commentator, and murmured the words and what he took to be the air of *The Red-Haired Man's Wife* until he felt a genital erection inside his trousers.

The programme changed: and the news bulletin began. Still murmuring the song, and stroking his body, he listened with less than half an ear to mutilation in Belfast, villainy in Rhodesia, corruption in Washington, mysterious goings-on amongst the leadership of Fianna Fáil, and some rubbish about the Bishop of Cashel. Then he heard the word "Galway". What — Galway — what was it . . . ? "After the demonstration, a spokesman for the local Gardaí had stated that the trouble was now contained and the women who had been taken away had since" — had since — *what* . . . ? "been released . . . ?" Or had they? Jackson hadn't been listening properly. What women? Taken away? What the bloody hell had happened? He jumped up and began to sweat. Should he get in the boat and go ashore to find out? There was a telephone box two miles away up the boreen, but he'd have to walk because Fionnuala of course had taken the car. And the phone was always out of order in that damned box — the drunks out of Feeny's Bar used to jam the slot with bent coins every night trying to call for taxis to get them home, damn the bloody drunks, it was always out of order. And besides, wasn't it bloody rough out there on the lake, and his outboard not working? Besides, it was dark. If she had been released, she'd be back the next morning. But was it her? God knows there were enough women in Galway fit to be 'taken away' by the Guards. God knows some of them needed it. He could make an absolute public monkey out of himself panicking like this. When was the next news bulletin? They had one at the end of the night's programme, didn't they? So he waited, still sweating, till the end of the night's programme. Twice he went and emptied himself — his bowels running like a tap — on the chemical closet round the back of the cabin in the lean-to.

The bulletin again. He put his ear to the radio, and his hands trembled. Belfast, Rhodesia, Washington, the Bishop of Cashel. Fianna Fáil had slipped to fifth place — apparently the rumours about Haughey were unfounded. Then Sport, motor-accidents — but nothing, but nothing at all about Galway. God, he'd imagined it. Hadn't he? Well, even if he hadn't, it couldn't be that important. Surely nothing important could happen in so small a country and RTE not pick it up and enlarge upon it — but they hadn't. He'd go to bed. Yes, bed. God in Heaven, what the hell had that fool of a woman been up to? He knew it, he knew it, he knew it. *O'Reilly* an ultra-leftist? In the name of — of all manner of archaic ridiculous blasphemy — what in the name of *anything* could we call that unbelievable Maeve? He went to bed, growling, maintaining himself wronged. He slept, after more wine: and he dreamed.

He saw the lake, flat, windless, in the middle of the night. It was raining. It was raining so hard that the smooth water was pitted all over like smallpox — he had once seen a child in India in a village infected with smallpox, not a smooth place anywhere upon the poor little brown face, black eruptions on every inch. It was pitch dark and yet he could see everything. Out of the water arose a dark lump, no, not a lump, more like a column, it rose up, it was moving slowly towards the shore. It splashed as it came, growing taller all the time. It was a woman. She was naked, with long black hair streaked all down around her flanks, wet, shining under the clouded sky where there was neither moon nor star to make anything shine. She had two eyes as white as water underneath her black fringe, and a huge mouth wide open with water running out of it. He had a fearsome feeling that there were also two eyes looking out at him from the thick mat of her pubic hair, and the mouth beneath them was also wide open — certainly there was a white stream of water running down between her legs as she walked. She was clear of the lake and coming up the grassy gleaming strand of the island, walking slowly upon tip-toe. In her forehead was a silver fork: stuck deep into the pale brow up to the roots of the prongs.

Then the dark became dark again — how could it be anything else when there were clouds across both moon and stars? He saw the woman no more; and he heard only the continuing rainfall.

He was in the cabin, on his bunk, and the rainfall roared on the roof. He was sitting naked on his bunk, and cold, cold as the lake itself, he was trembling all over and unable even to reach out his arm for his clothes. All his bedding was wet, and there were puddles between the bed and the door, they shone in the moonlight that flooded in at the window — but there were clouds across the moon, so how could there be moonlight? He looked at the puddles. Some of them were near his bed, some of them near the door — but most of them to one side all round the base of the little narrow door that opened into a cupboard where fishing-rods were sometimes kept. Neither Jackson nor Fionnuala fished: but the previous owner of the island had done little else, and the furnishings of the cabin were all for the furtherance of immeasurable murder of trout. This door was about twelve inches wide and six feet tall, and the cupboard could contain whole fasces of rods, standing erect in the shadows, all ready for instant use. Jackson discovered his own phallus in such a condition, though never in his life had he felt less venereal. Was it possible that a man could become tumescent through sheer fear? He had always believed that the opposite should be the case.

What the devil was in that cupboard? There was water leaking out of it, drop drop drop down the low sill onto the boards of the floor. With a strenuous effort he spread his feet upon the floor, took one step, then two, stretched out his arm, and pulled open the cupboard. She was in there, stark naked, with the fork in her head. Her mouth was now closed.

He looked at her, rigid. She looked back at him and there were no pupils to her white eyes. She stood stiffly upright: and he slowly became aware that a greeny-white trickle of what ought to have been blood was coming down from the prongs of the fork, down either side of her flat nose, down her chin, onto her chest. It was not a large trickle, but it was continuous and ran all down her body, between her small breasts, over her belly, down the inside of her thighs, continuous, to seep out of the cupboard, over the doorsill, throughout the whole cabin.

She did not open her mouth; but he was sure he heard her speak. It was as though she spoke between torrents of water. He could hardly distinguish the words, they were so confused with the wet noise. "It was yourself sank down the fork till it came into the flesh of my head: and I have come to bring it back."

He returned to his senses — or awoke — or recovered — he could not be certain exactly which it was — the following morning, after daybreak. He was very cold and his body ached all over. He must have been lying on the hard plank floor all night. He had every symptom of a bad hangover. He dressed himself clumsily, unable to remember anything, except that he was on the island and Fionnuala had left him. But what for? And for how long? He could not fix his mind clearly enough to sort it out. He tried to put on his shoes and dropped one of them. He picked it up, and picked up a fork that was lying untidily under the corner of his bunk. He put the fork on the table, put the shoe first on the wrong foot, then on the right one, and went over to the door. He opened it and looked out. It was beautiful weather, though the thorn leaves and the grass were soaking wet as though it had rained all night. The outline of the mountains at the top of the lake was so clear that it might have been painted by a sixteenth-century Indian miniaturist. There was a lot of water in patches around his feet on the floor of the cabin. Of course the roof had always leaked. Then he heard an outboard motor — he must in fact have been hearing it for some time: because even as he noticed it, it cut out. A boat was coming in to land beside his own boat at the island's small pier. It was a strange boat, larger than the standard lake-skiffs, with a bigger outboard than usual, and it was painted an unrelieved black. There were three men in it — one of them in the tweed cap and nondescript jacket of the local boatmen, the other two in dark uniforms. They were Civic Guards. The boat grounded on the strand and the two Guards scrambled out, carefully, taking good care not to get any splashes of water into the tops of their wellingtons.

Jackson remained standing in the doorway of his little house: he watched them as they came solemnly up the green shining slope. The first Guard was a Sergeant, a solid hard professional heavyweight with very sharp blue eyes. He sent these blue eyes in every direction, taking in the cabin, the island, the trees, the birds, the flowers, Jackson's own boat, the tins of rat poison under the joists of the house. The last thing he looked at was Jackson. He said something, at length. "We endeavoured to take her in for her own protection, d'you see, sir, but there is no doubt the crowd was aroused. Not a matter, d'you see, sir, of convenience to the Guards on duty. And we judged it best at the time to make no statement to the Press or the radio representatives. The blow she was struck could easily have been harmless: but the doctor at the Regional Hospital said something about a vital place, like it might have been oh a chançe in two hundred — bedad the man hadn't even screwed his fist into a ball. Being poked as it were with the bend of his knuckles. But the Regional Hospital said internal, a vital place, d'you see, sir. Oh there's no doubt at all, sir, that the Guard who held her is exonerated — how the divil could he know that the only way back to the Barracks would be filled up by certain elements. The poor fellow had no choice but to fetch her, so, through the thick of the crowd, and they hostile. You'll be making your own arrangements about the funeral, I suppose. Would you say now your — your wife — would that be correct, sir? Would you say she was a Catholic? There are arrangements fair enough for the Protestants in the Galway cemetery, but if it's not a religious burial, bedad, I've no notion indeed how you'll manage at all at all. . . . Her friend, Miss Hanratty — er — her friend, I forget the full name — her friend was after making the very divil of a hullabaloo: but I think we have her settled by now, if you want to talk to her. Will we give you a lift over?"

The other Guard, who had not yet said anything, was a tall thin bitter young man with a swart pointed face like an eagle. He uttered what seemed — incredibly — to be a screech of laughter. "Sure he has his own boat. If we took him in ours, wouldn't his own be left on the island for the divil and all his dogs to be coming over to collect afterwards, he'd never get the dispositions right in all the confusion — let him take his own boat, Sergeant, and if he's not fit to row her himself, let Sean Riordan go with him to see her beached and properly tied-up." Sean Riordan must have been the civilian in the dark brown tweed jacket.

Silently they climbed into the boats and shoved off. Sean Riordan made no attempt to start Jackson's motor, but set to the oars with the practiced skill of a regular lake-dwelling man. Jackson, in the stern, sat as dumb as a fish and stared at him as he pulled. The tweed jacket gaped to the movement. Jackson saw an underarm holster and the butt of an automatic. Sean Riordan was no boatman, but a Branchman in plain clothes. Sean Riordan's voice was hoarse and by no means expressive. He paused between phrases to give himself breath as he rowed. "Certain elements in these times — oh a terrible deal of difficulty. You'll understand, Mr. Jackson, the outsiders in the community have their own place and their own welcome here. When all's said, 'tis a difficult matter. Your — your wife, now: they tell me, in the first place, from Dublin? And you yourself, would it be Birmingham?"

"No," said Jackson, "no, I was born in York. As a matter of fact."

Sean Riordan pulled the oars for another hundred yards or so. Then he showed all his teeth, in what might have been a smile, but was not. "Don't you think you should go home?" Jackson made a movement towards him — a movement of vehemence, almost of violence. Sean Riordan's hands were off the oars in an instant, and his right hand towards his armpit. But Jackson was still again and the hand stopped in mid-air. There was a noise in Jackson's throat that rose up and was cut away. Maybe the Branchman never understood it, but Jackson had in fact spoken. He had said — or had attempted to say — "God shut up your mouth, man — I *am* at home!" Then he fell forward from the thwart into the bottom of the boat and slumped down heavily on the sodden cushion which still lay where he had kicked it the previous afternoon.

HARRY HARRISON

All Wheels, Gears and Cogs

"All wheels, gears and cogs, that's what it was, sergeant, standing outside my window in a driving rain, just hulking there as dark as Satan. Jayzus! I could only stare, paralysed I was, and then the lightning flashed and I could see it clear as day, clear as seeing you across this table. I crossed myself, me! Like any old woman passing a church. It was big as you, bigger, just standing there in the rain and dripping with water from every wheel and rod. I fell backward, the sight was that horrible, as though I had been smote across the chest. And then — it was gone. With more courage than I ever thought myself possessing I willed myself back to the window and saw this sinister shape fleeing across the fields. Running steadily and straight — and do I have to tell in which direction it was running, sergeant?"

"If you're not telling I won't be knowing, will I, Sean?" the Sergeant said in his slow and plodding, official and careful way. Sean shifted his slight weight from one foot to the other, wriggled his nose like a rabbit, which he did resemble in many ways, and jingled the loose change in his pocket while he waited for the policeman's slow words to rumble leisurely by.

"You know which direction without my telling, for you have heard this story before from more than one and have chosen, in the majesty of the law, to ignore all the warnings. You'll heed mine now! It went *that* way — towards Dun Dubhe. So what do you intend to do about it?"

"I intend to speak to the baron since yours is indeed not the first report I have had of unusual doings near the Black Tower." The Sergeant rose slowly to his feet, carefully buttoning his collar with fingers thick as black puddings. He was a big, strong man was the sergeant, and needed no weapon other than these great hands to quell the wildest of donnybrooks at closing time at the pub on Saturday nights.

"Though no harm has been done to any person or property to my knowledge, there have been complaints."

"And about time, too," Sean said, scuttling out of the way of the thudding boots. "Sure and I'd come with you except I have important business elsewhere."

"Indeed," the Sergeant rumbled noncommittaly as he locked the door to the Gárda station and climbed majestically aboard his large black push-bike. "Indeed," and rolled off down the road in the direction of the Black Tower.

It has been said, and truthfully enough, if there is a place where strange things might best be seen it surely is in this part of North Mayo. Ireland has desolate moors and windswept bogs from coast to coast, but nothing like the barren forsakenness of this corner of the land. Like the moon, though green, but still as empty as the moon. A landscape that goes on forever, without a tree to break its emptiness, slashed by sharp cliffs and wicked inlets torn into by the sea. No place for men — yet men live here, have lived here, and in all this emptiness there are still crumbling, torn ruins that go back to the beginning of history and beyond.

The Black Tower was one of these. It stood hard by the ruins of a small church and a tiny churchyard, the church roofless and filled with nettles and brambles, scattered with gray skulls that had worked up from the soil below. Above this grim scene the tower stood, even grimmer. Local legends about it were many and varied, though invariably sinister. But what was true was that it was now occupied — and an object of intense interest to the people about, as well being a source of darkest speculation. The Sergeant had heard all of the stories and had nodded and listened and remembered and had apparently done nothing. But who was to follow him on the blackest nights through the twisting paths, where a single misstep could suck the unwary down into the bottomless bog? If he had been up this rutted track before he gave no sign; if he had seen anything before this day of interest in the grim black tower he did not reveal it. Yet he had come this evening, with the red sunset to his back, and he must have had his reasons. Carefully and precisely he leaned his bicycle against the crumbling stone wall, turned and knocked with hard knuckles on old wood.

He had to knock twice more, ever patient, before there were slow footsteps inside, followed by a great rattling and clattering of hidden chains. Then the door opened a crack and a wary eye peered suspiciously out.

"Good evening," the Sergeant said in tones that revealed naught.

"What you want?" a hollow voice said.

"To have a few words with you, if you please. May I come in?"

The eye blinked rapidly, then vanished from the crack and the door closed. There was more rattling before the portal opened again, wider this time, and the Sergeant walked slowly in. He watched calmly while the man closed the door and turned about, a thin cadaverous man with pale skin and yellowed eye, wispy white hair falling about any which way. His clothes were old-fashioned and rusty; heavy chains crossed and recrossed his waistcoat. With stern fixed gaze the Sergeant spoke again.

"You are Mr. Vanstroge?" he asked.

"No. I am Baron VonStroj. And your business is . . .?"

"The present tenant of this establishment?"

"I am, I am! What do you want?" The baron was getting nervous, his thin white fingers flapping like empty gloves.

"It is my duty to inform you, baron, that there have been reports from the people in the village of strange doings in this establishment . . ."

"What is strange doings! I am a simple bachelor, I cook, I care for myself, read a book, bother no one."

"Is that so? Then what of the large laboratory behind that door?" The arm went out, the finger pointed, as strong and steady as a jabbing spear.

All the strength was drained from the baron on the instant. He staggered back as though from a blow, seeking support from a small table, knocking over the glass-cased skeleton of a bat that adorned it, all unknowing. "Is lie . . ." was all he could gasp.

"Is it? Then you won't mind I am sure if I have a look for myself."

In two mighty strides the Sergeant was at the door, his hand on the handle, turning.

"No! Is locked!"

It may have been. It meant nothing to this hand, that arm. A sudden twist and it was open — bits of metal rattling down inside the locking mechanism. Swung wide, the door opening was like the curtain parting on a stage. The secret was revealed.

A laboratory. Shining steel, glinting chrome, sparkling

glass, so out of keeping with the dark stone walls. Gleaming machines of unknown purpose, control panels multifaced with dials. Wheels, levers, knobs, wires, tubes, insulators with shining rods rising from them up which climbed great crackling ladders of sparks to burst and explode. The baron's shuffling steps followed the Sergeant's solid ones into the room, the wispy voice wispier still in the cavernous room.

"A simple hobby, no more. Innocent experiments to pass the long hours . . ."

"You have lied to me once, baron. I would not advise doing that again. People have reported to me sightings of a strange and inhuman creature in this vicinity. More than one person has reported it moving in this direction. Would you be knowing anything about that?"

The answer at first was only a gasp, and when the words themselves finally came they were no more than a whisper.

"Lies. They wish to make trouble for me, a foreigner in a strange land. They watch too much television late in the evening, bad films that make lies about my homeland . . ."

"You are in trouble, baron." With each word spoken the man flinched back as though it were a blow. Once again the finger pointed. "Would you tell me what stands behind that curtain there — or should I see for myself?"

"You can't . . . you mustn't . . ." the baron gulped feebly, but made no motion to stop the man. One, two, three and the Sergeant was across the room and taking hold of the curtain. It came down in a fine cloud of dust that settled softly in the silence. The Sergeant did not move nor utter a word, but a keen glance would have surely detected a glimmering light of victory in that steely eye.

The thing was huge. Metallic and shining. All wheels, gears and cogs, cams and levers and devices strange to the normal eye. Its head was roughly in the place a man's head might have been, but its features were no more than metallic parts in an arrangement without human meaning.

"This is your creature," the Sergeant said in a voice that both questioned and pronounced judgement. "I have seen it before and I have seen it come here. I do not believe the stories the old wives tell that it is the first of many, that you are building an army of satanic creatures that will sweep mankind into the sea, take over the world. Nor do I believe the babbling of fools who say you have brought this machine from another world, another dimension, and that it is the first of hordes to come. I do not believe these things as I did not believe the lies you told me when I entered here. It is time for the truth at last. You will speak."

The precision of the toneless words, like beats on a muffled drum, drove the baron back and down, destroyed any capacity for free will that he might have had left. With the greatest of efforts he drew himself up, shuddering, then shuffled forward.

"The truth . . . of course . . . I must tell the truth."

The unsteady fingers found a switch high up on the metallic creature and threw it. Motors began to whine within it and lights flashed on. There were clattering sounds as gears engaged and the creature rumbled forward slowly into the room. It went past the Sergeant who turned to watch it, his face as expressionless as the machine's. The baron tottered after and found the switch that stopped it.

"This is the truth . . . I beg you not to reveal it." He drew himself up a bit, making some attempt to restore the fragments of vanished dignity. "I was not without power, money, in my homeland, before the present regime reduced me to what you see now. In my youth I was well known as an amateur prestidigitator and was in great demand at parties. Not for money — never! My rank would not permit that. At the noble homes of dear friends. Now, in my old age, I hoped to turn that youthful skill to some advantage, to change my name so those old friends still alive will not die of shame, to attempt to earn a poor living upon the commercial stage. I have made this creature and it will do wondrous things . . ."

"I would like to see a wondrous thing."

The baron hesitated at this, then moved slowly to the machine. A number of adjustments were made and a button finally pressed. The creature stirred to life, lights flashing on and off while a thin tune like that of an electronic music box sounded from its interior. It took hesitant steps forward and back in time with the music and, when the music had ended and the dance was over, it stopped and sounded a hoarse whistle, while at the same time unfurling a flag from the top of its head. But the mechanism jammed and the tiny flagstaff snapped and the flag fell to the floor in a jumble of sleazy fabric. The Sergeant looked down at it for a silent moment, then spoke.

"That was not a very wondrous thing," said he. "Nor am I pleased with this device for it seems shabbily made, see where that part has fallen off, and if demonstrated in public it could be dangerous to the spectators. A licence will be needed . . ."

"No! I beg of you. Officialdom would not permit it. They are all against me. I will show you, promise not to reveal, no machine licence is needed — see!"

The baron threw back the clasps in the machine's rear then opened a door there and snapped his fingers. A small man in worn coveralls climbed out and bowed towards the sergeant. He was wizened and bald and looked as tired as the baron.

The Sergeant looked from one of them to the other, then to the opening in the machine and the tiny seat inside and the handles and wheels that made it go.

Then he smiled, a strange sight on that stone face. Yet it was a smile, gone as fast as it had come. And the Sergeant was gone as well, satisfied, his domain still safe, his people unthreatened. Heavy footsteps were followed by a slam of the door.

"We are safe," the baron said. "The fools suspect nothing." His fingers went to the back of the small man's neck and pulled downward. The flesh parted bloodlessly and from the opening there stepped a tiny machine man, almost a replica of the other and larger one before them.

"We are safe," the machine said tonelessly. "The others can now come."

He reached up and helped the baron to open the flesh at the back of his neck so he too could emerge.

KYRIL BONFIGLIOLI

As Simple As That

Our small twins were little bleeders. That is to say, they were born with haemophilia, a rare condition which prevents the blood from clotting, so that a bruise is a disaster and the least scratch a major calamity. It is inherited only through the female side but girls are hardly ever born with it; if they are, they do not survive puberty, of course. Our children's names were Timothy and Theresa.

It is neither an easy nor a happy task to bring up haemophiliac children but my wife had all the love and strength in the world and we learned to entrench ourselves into a pattern of life adapted to the daily nightmare, the constant terror. It was rather like a war in which all nature was our adversary and in which we had no weapons but constant vigilance, continual fear. We lay down at night with those and they greeted us in the dawn.

Every father's pride at watching his son climbing a tree for the very first time must be mixed with a gut-clenching fear that the boy will fall; every mother dies a little death when her child comes home with a leg gashed and bloody from some careless encounter with a barbed-wire fence. Our kids would never, ever, be able to savour the delights of climbing a tree, nor could they approach a barbed-wire fence no matter what adventures lay on the further side. They could not even forage through brambles for fat blackberries.

Children are wonderfully resilient: our Timmy and Terry grew up within the elaborate system of taboos with which we had to surround them and they accepted their difference from other kids just as though it were all part of some grisly Grimm's fairy tale. It was something to be taken just as lightly as the stories — but just as seriously, too, as all magic must be taken.

I would not describe myself as a sentimental man — sentiment was not at a premium where I was raised — but I must admit that there were times when I could have wept at hearing our little bleeders pattering out the speech we had drilled into them as soon as they could string the words together:

"How do you do," they would chant in chorus, "we're supposed to tell you that we're bleeders and so we mustn't play rough games eckseckera because if we get bruised inside or cut outside we might die of it. It's called hiffomilia."

Well, we coped. We scraped and saved every penny so that we might one day emigrate to Western Australia and buy a little place near a sandy beach where Timmy and Terry could play without too much danger. No; when I say that *we* coped, I am lying. It was my wife who coped quietly, capably, whilst I dramatised, flung my arms about, cursed Heaven and formulated a new and wilder plan every day of the week. Of course I worked; I worked like a madman, boasting incessantly of the money I was stuffing into our "Australia-or-bust" bank-account. I really believed that I was the strong man, the capable man, the man who was going to solve all problems by working just that little longer each day, squeezing out that extra 1 per cent commission; shouldering my weedy competitors out of the field. "No friends, can't afford them; never give a sucker an even break" — you know the silly rubbish. The dirty taste still lingers in my mouth. God, how I worked, though. When I came home at night I had just the courage left to play jokes with the kids; just the courage to tell my wife I loved her, the courage to lie that I had already eaten and the courage to clump up to bed with a half a bottle of whisky inside me. Sometimes I took a shower, sometimes I forgot. The worst times were when I ran the shower while I brushed my teeth, splashed a little water on my hair and pretended I had showered. My wife never gave any least hint of disbelief or disapproval. I suppose she knew I was doing my best and she was too loyal to face the fact that my best was not good enough. (The only loyalty I can return to her is to continue to call her 'my wife', rather than to use her name. Privacy is almost the last coin a bum has in his pocket.)

It was not until she died that I understood how utterly I had been living off her quiet strength, how shabby and how small had been my money-scrabbling contribution. Indeed, when I say that 'she died' I know that I am piddling with words. Certainly she died. Equally certainly, I killed her. No, there was no coal-hammer, kitchen-knife or hatchet — my worst enemy (well, yes, *me* of course), might charge me with self-pity but hardly with vulgarity — nor was there, of course, any murderous intent.

The 'deodand' or instrument of death was my two-year old

saloon which was fifteen hundred miles overdue for a service. Inside the saloon was me; inside me was two-thirds of a bottle of whisky. Beside me, until I hit the stone-work of the bridge, was my wife.

I had not realised quite how much I loved her until the surgeon came to tell me that she was dead. He was a decent enough man; he would not meet my eyes because he wanted to spare me the contempt which I would have seen in his. (I like to think that he was being compassionate but sometimes at night I think of the animals in the zoo: have you noticed that they never look at us? They have seen a great many of us and have not been impressed.)

Just what does one do in such a situation? For a childless coward there would have been an easy solution of course, but there were the children. They were there. I don't mean that they had been in the car, I just mean that they were there, existing, alive, sure that they belonged to me and that I belonged to them. So, the first dirty job I had to set myself to do was to tell lies to my children. They had not been told lies before. I let myself into the house and heard their grandmother reading *The House at Pooh Corner* to them. I stole into the junk-room which I used to call my study, unlocked the tantalus and poured myself a massive drink. It smelt of blood; I carried it into the lobby and poured it down the sink. In the kitchen I found some cold coffee, black and bitter. I drank it all. Then I went upstairs.

The kids were a little frightened at my damaged face at first but I wiggled my fingers at them and they knew it was me. While they laughed and cried and asked a hundred questions I was able to lock eyes with the grandmother for an instant and give her that fleeting closure of the eyelids, that infinitesimal shake of the head which all old ladies understand. Old ladies know about death, it's the only hobby left to them.

Then I told lies to my children.

I told them that their mother had gone to find a lovely new house for us all and that for a few days I would be putting them to bed myself — how they laughed! — and that my face was all funny and black-and-blue because I had captured a naughty bandit and marched him off to the Police Station. I explained that I was so late because I had walked home: I was tired of our old car and had decided to buy a nice new one. Their grandmother nearly spoiled it all by bursting into tears but Timothy and Theresa paid little attention: even the littlest children know that grannies are nice but *silly*. Timmy was eager to know what kind of a motor-car the new one would be; Terry, bless her, was much more concerned about the naughty man I had marched to the Police Station: would they give him a proper, hot supper? With cocoa? And a comfy bed? I reassured her on all three counts. Lying, even to children, comes amazingly easy with a little practice. The practice is what hurts. Once you are expert you have nothing to fear but sleepless nights — and you can buy a remedy for those at any public house.

I have to say that the grandmother — she was my wife's mother, not mine — held us all together like a hoop of steel in the ensuing days. Neither by look nor word did she reproach me for killing her daughter and the loving concern she gave to Timmy and Terry was no greater than what she spent on me. Not once did she coax or bully me to eat — but whenever I strayed into the kitchen there always happened to be a dish of bacon and eggs or corned-beef-hash or a nice little pie keeping warm on the hot-plate, with a hot roll wrapped in a napkin and some neat curls of butter in a bowl of cracked ice. We 'passed no remarks' about such things. I forget whether I said that she was an Irishwoman.

Of an evening she would come and sit with me in the study — the drawing-room seemed nowadays too large — and would knit quietly while I pretended to read. She never seemed to be watching me but every once in a while, at precisely the right moment, she would say that if I should be fancying a little nip of something she might just take the least little tincture herself. Looking back on those dreadful days now, I seem to recall that the bottle always held a couple of stiff drinks for me as well as the little 'tincture' she would take; never more, never less. I suppose that she was, in a quiet way, rather a wonderful old lady. Certainly, she must have loved her daughter very much to have been so unremittingly patient with me, her daughter's husband. I mean, she can scarcely have liked me. Have I said that she was an Irishwoman? There were many things I did not understand in those days.

I was, of course, at my wits' end; there simply was not enough money for the Australian venture and the senior partner of my firm was beginning to make infinitely tactful noises about how fierce the competition was, how narrow our margin of profitability and so forth. I knew what he meant. He meant that the firm could not afford to carry passengers and that I had become a passenger. We had a chat; he bought out my holding of shares at a more than generous price and the Board of Directors gave me six months' salary and a lump sum based on my commission earned in the previous year. I do not mean to denigrate their generosity when I say that they probably felt that getting rid of what I had become was cheap at the price.

The children's grandmother — somehow I have never thought of her as my mother-in-law — seemed to do no coaxing nor persuading but one day I found myself on the ferry to Ireland, with Timothy and Theresa bouncing and laughing in the back seat of the new car. I remember a pleasant little hotel with a French name in Dún Laoghaire, then an eighty-miles drive to a grand old house in an overgrown park somewhere deep in County Cavan. We were expected: the owner of the house had been at school with the children's grandmother. Timmy and Terry were whisked away by a fat and kindly housekeeper of the sort who loves to feed little children and tell them bed-time stories; I was given a searching glare from two of the bluest eyes I have ever seen, one large glass of Scotch and the most comfortable bed I have ever slept in. There was a dish on the bedside table containing three different kinds of biscuits; I had not realised that there were still houses like that.

I spent most of the next day in bed. People brought me things to eat on trays. The children, I was assured, were occupied with ponies and puppies. I got up in time for the ritual of watching them have their bath then the grand old lady showed me the library, a library which would have aroused envy in the breast of a saint. There was a pair of leaves from a

Codex Aureus of the Ninth Century, Wynkyn de Worde's 1498 printing of the Canterbury Tales, both of the Shakespeare folios — and a thousand other things which no collector today could afford. In the modern section I noticed that all the better things from 1920 onwards were affectionately inscribed to a lady, using her pet name, and I realised with a blush that I should have realised that the owner of the startling blue eyes had been very well known to the world under her maiden name.

She saw my expression change and she laughed happily. "Yes, I know," she said, "you thought I had died long ago. No, don't pretend; come and have some dinner. Then you must get an early night if you are to get to Galway by lunchtime."

I need scarcely say that dinner was of a robust splendour no longer seen in England except at the High Tables of one or two of the better Oxford Colleges.

"Galway?" I asked mildly over the *Potage Printanière,* "Am I going to Galway in the morning?"

"Galway," she replied firmly in the sort of voice which brooks no contradiction. "There is a beach there where no one goes; a half-mile semi-circle of soft shell-sand, precisely what your children need. I have spoken today on the telephone with a reliable person there who sells property; he has just the place for you and at a price you can afford." I opened my mouth, then shut it again. She would know. By way of keeping my end up, so to say, I observed that some of the 16th and 17th Century books in the library should be shelved with the fore-edge outward rather than the spine and cited Earle's *Microcosmographia* to support my view. She knew all about Earle and this led us on to Clarendon and the dinner progressed with an added relish of bookish lore.

Our coffee was brought to us in the library where I was allowed to dote on a couple of Grolier bindings, then I was awarded a handsome half-tumbler of Smith's Glenlivet and, in the most tactful way you can imagine, packed off to bed.

"I shall not be up when you leave," she said, "but you will be called at the proper hour, your motor will be in front of the house and there will of course be a hamper of necessities in it. Your children are looking forward to their jaunt." I tried to make a little speech of thanks but was quelled by a daunting glance from those terrifying blue eyes.

"Goodnight," is what I said in the end, "and, ah, thank you." She bowed, but only from the neck of course.

In the morning I had no hangover: hangovers are for people who have not had a proper dinner. On my breakfast tray there was a sketch-map of my route and the name of the reliable person who sold property. The fat and kindly housekeeper had the children waiting for me at the motor-car; they seemed plumper and happier than I had seen them for weeks. I tried to slip a fiver into the housekeeper's hand but she explained, in the gentlest way, that it was not the custom of the house.

At the main gates an old man was pushing a bicycle laden with saggans. Having studied the customs of the country I lifted an index-finger from the wheel in salute. I couldn't quite catch what he said but it sounded like "May God be good to youse". The kids waved to him cheerfully from the back seat: a glance in my rear-view mirror showed me that he was waving his hat at them and that his nut-brown face was split with a friendly grin. I shall never understand the Irish.

We made good speed to our destination but we lost ourselves once or twice so at lunchtime we drew up just outside Ballykeeran on the shore of Lough Ree and explored the luncheon-hamper. There was a nice little chicken, each dissected part neatly put up in waxed paped (it was not the sort of house to have heard of Clingfilm), crisp rolls, a crock of buttercup-yellow butter, some hard-boiled eggs, some *pâté* sandwiches, the hearts of three lettuces — icy-cold in a big Thermos — a quart bottle of lemonade *made of lemons* and, bless the grand old lady, a capacious flask of the Glenlivet for me. Out of some well of self-respect I dredged up the courage to have no more than one single sip, washed down with the capital lemonade. The housekeeper, bless her heart, had even remembered to include a damp face-cloth for wiping sticky little fingers.

Much heartened by this repast from times long vanished, I zoomed through Athlone and Ballinasloe and, quite early in the afternoon, made my rendezvous with the 'person who sold property'. I had been a little worried about this because his name, clearly written on my piece of paper, was J. Mac Seosamh and I hadn't the first notion of how to pronounce it. I need not have worried; he was one of those huge, pink extroverts who squeeze your hand until it's numb, pat your children on the head and sell you things before you have time to clear your throat. Well, I knew how to deal with that sort of thing: in my career as a businessman I had sold more people more things that they hadn't known they wanted than this fellow had eaten hot dinners. What vexed me about him was his frantic desire to play the stage-Irishman for the delectation of the British twit. Me. After a few 'begob's' and 'Jasus, Mary and Joseph's' I lost patience, took his arm and drew him a few yards along the pavement.

"At any moment," I said carefully, "you are going to say 'begorrah'. If you do, I shall spit in your eye. O.K.?" He looked at me blankly, then his great, ham-like face split into an enormous grin. "I'm sorry, Sorr, but the tourists expect it, you see that, don't you?"

"I am not a tourist," I said. "And my name is not 'Sorr', it's John. What's yours?" He looked shy; then defiant.

"Jesse," he said.

"Bloody good name. Now, just over the street there I see a pub called Hughie somebody's. Does he draw a good glass of stout?"

"He does."

"Then why are we standing here like a pair of idiots?"

In the pub, the licensee — I already knew enough not to say the word 'landlord' for it's still a dirty word in Ireland — proved to be one of those sour, mistrustful bachelors who pretend to hate everyone but who know how to draw a pint of stout. I bought the kids a bottle each of some awful fizzy stuff — and looked askance at the chipped edges of their glasses.

"Straws, please," I murmured. The publican glared at me.

"No straws. Dis isn't a Select Bar. Yer not in Dublin now."

I didn't know how to deal with that. Jesse Mac Seosamh did. He leant over the bar in a friendly way and stared at the publican.

"Straws," he murmured. The publican met his gaze, wavered, went to a sort of a hatchway and screamed down it.

"Ye lazy idle scuts," he screamed, "why is there no straws in the house?" Straws arrived, both plain and coloured, before Jesse and I had even penetrated the 'clerical collars' of our pints of porter. I remember thinking this a little strange at the time but almost anything can happen in Ireland and, indeed, usually does.

Refreshed, we drove a few miles to the splendid, curving beach which has all that the heart could desire. On the way I felt confident enough to ask Jesse Mac Seosamh what the 'Seosamh' part of his name meant and how it was to be spoken. "Just 'Joseph'," he said. At the farthest end of the southern arm of the beach there was an old planting of trees sheltering an extraordinary house which looked like a Scottish shooting-box of Balmoral vintage crossed with a Tyrolean hunting-lodge. It was quite enchantingly silly — I wanted it. Before we got out of the car I coaxed the asking-price out of Mac Joseph; it was very low, well within my means, but he warned me that it would need quite that amount again spent on it. I could see that.

A monstrous key squeaked and grated the side door open and I told the kids that they might explore but to take care. They trotted off through the cobwebs and dust-sheets while Jesse and I prodded broom-handles against sagging ceilings, poked pen-knives into suspect woodwork and sniffed knowledgeably for damp-rot. The fabric was not much worse than he had said and he told me that he had a nephew who was the best carpenter in the West.

We were walking towards the main part of the house when Timmy and Terry came pelting out, their faces radiant. I fielded them with my arms and told them to steady up.

"Oh Daddy," they yelled, "you never told us it was a surprise! It's the house that Mummy went to find for us, isn't it?" I found myself at a loss for words and Jesse was no help. Tactfully he turned his back and stared out of a window.

"What makes you think that, sillies?" I grunted.

"Oh, Daddy, she's here, you know she is, we saw her, we saw her, she's upstairs, up the big curly stairs, she's standing there, oh do come on, Daddy."

Jesse came to my aid this time, he must have seen the colour leave my face. He took my arm and said "Come along, John" or something like that and the children tugged us into the hall. There was indeed a lovely curly staircase leading up to a sort of mezzanine or gallery but no one stood there.

"We couldn't go up the stairs, Daddy; Mummy wouldn't let us, she sort of waved her hands up and down to say we mustn't go up; she probably wanted to say something secret to you first."

I looked imploringly at Jesse: he gave me back the look which a sergeant gives a young officer, the look which says that it is *you* have a brass pip on your shoulder-strap. I pounded up the stairs, waving at the kids. I was almost halfway up when the whole thing cracked and crumbled under my feet, my right leg smashed through a rotten tread which ripped my thigh to rashers as I saved myself by a grab at the balustrade. Jesse, good man that he was, coaxed the kids out to the car before extricating my bloody leg from the rotten splinters of woodwork. The femoral artery was intact, of course, or I would not be here to tell the tale, but I bled like a stuck pig. I remember him taking off my shirt and ripping it into bandages before I passed out. On the way to the cottage hospital I came to my senses once or twice and heard him cheering up the children.

As I passed in and out of consciousness I heard snatches of conversation.

"Of course your mam was there," said Jesse. "Why wouldn't she be and with that rotten old staircase to keep you from?"

"I think my mother is dead," said Timothy.

"And what difference does that make?" Even Timmy couldn't answer that one.

A few days later we all met in the little town: the children were full of food and fun. They had been staying with lovely ladies.

"The good nuns have been looking after them," said Jesse.

"They were *not* nuns," said Theresa, "they were Carmelites. And Daddy, would you believe it, Saint Theresa is under the special protection of their own patron?"

"Fancy that," I said in a flat voice.

Jesse accepted a lift home.

"About that house," I said diffidently. He glanced at me.

"We both of us know that you can never go there again," he said. "It did its work." We drove a little further, towards where I supposed he lived.

"And I don't think," he said, "that I have any other properties to offer on the shore of Galilee just now."

"On the shore of *what*?"

"Galway." I must have misheard him, obviously. We dropped him at the entrance to an overgrown lane. I knew better than to offer him anything for his time and trouble. Feebly, I said "That nephew of yours, the carpenter, is he in the yellow pages?"

"You'll find him alright," he said.

We drove off.

"Daddy," said Theresa, "you never asked me who was the patron, the *real* patron of the Carmelite ladies." I pulled myself together.

"Saint Cunegonde?" I asked. "Saint Paula the Bearded? Surely not Saint Kyril, who cruelly murdered the female mathematician Hypatia?"

"Oh, do stop showing off, Daddy, make a proper guess." It wasn't a guess at all, of course; I just hadn't wanted to say it.

"St. Joseph?"

They clapped their hands, proud of me. That was the last time that anyone was proud of me. It was almost exactly nine years ago.

I am a childless man now, of course. I'm told that you can survive for years on a diet of self-pity and whisky. I still shave three times a week. That's in good weeks, of course.

Naturally, I cannot believe in God. But as sure as I'm sitting here and as deadly sure as you are scanning these lines, I believe in a big, kindly, pink fellow in County Galway who went by the name of J. Mac Joseph.

He is not in the telephone book.

FREDERICK FORSYTH

Used in Evidence

"You are not obliged to say anything, but anything you say will be taken down and may be used in evidence."

Part of the wording of the official caution, used in the British and Irish police forces by the cautioning officer to the suspect.

The big police car slid to a halt by the kerb some fifty feet from where the cordon spanned the street to keep the bystanders back. The driver kept the engine running, the wipers flicking rhythmically across the screen to push away the insistent drizzle. From the rear seat Chief Superintendent William J. Hanley looked forward through the glass to the groups of watchers outside the cordon and the knots of irresolute officials beyond it.

"Stay here," he told the driver and prepared to get out. The driver was pleased; the inside of the car was snug and warm, and he reasoned this was no morning to be walking up and down a slum street in the drifting rain. He nodded and cut the engine.

The precinct police chief slammed the door after him, hunched himself deeper into his dark blue overcoat and walked purposefully forward to the gap in the crowd barrier where a damp police officer watched over those who entered and left the cordoned area. Seeing Hanley he brought up a salute, stepped aside and let him pass through.

Big Bill Hanley had been twenty-seven years a policeman, starting by pounding the cobbled alleys of the Liberties and rising through the ranks to his present status. He had the build for it, over six feet and one inch of him and built like a truck. Thirty years before he was rated the best lock forward that ever came out of Athlone County; in his green Irish jersey he had been part of the best Rugby football team the country had ever produced, the team that Karl Mullen led to victory three years running in the Triple Crown and that wiped the floor with the English, the Welsh, the Scots and the French. That had not done his promotion chances any harm either, when he joined the force.

He liked the job; he got satisfaction from it, despite the poor pay and the long hours. But every job has its tasks that no one can enjoy, and this morning had brought one of them.

An eviction.

For two years, the Dublin City Council had been steadily demolishing the rash of tiny, back-to-back, one room up and one room down houses that formed the area known as the Gloucester Diamond.

Why it had ever been called that was a mystery. It had none of the wealth and privilege of the English royal House of Gloucester, nor any of the expensive brilliance of the diamond. Just an industrial slum lying behind the dockland zone on the north shore of the Liffey. Now most of it was flat, its dwellers re-housed in cubic council apartment blocks whose soul-numbing shapes could be seen half a mile away through the drizzle.

But it lay in the heart of Bill Hanley's precinct, so this morning's business was his responsibility, much as he hated it.

The scene between the twin chains of crowd barriers that cordoned the centre section of what had once been Mayo Road was as bleak that morning as the November weather. One side of the street was just a field of rubble, where soon the earth-movers would be at work, gouging out fresh foundations for the new shopping complex. The other side was the centre of attention. Up and down for hundreds of feet not a building stood. The whole area was flat as a pancake, the rain gleaming off the slick black tarmac of the new two-acre car park destined to house the vehicles of those who would one day work in the intended office blocks nearby. The entire two acres was fenced off by a nine-foot high chain-link fence; that is to say, almost the whole two acres.

Right in the centre, facing on to Mayo Road, was one single remaining house, like an old broken stump of tooth in a nice smooth gum. Either side of it the houses had been torn down, and each side of the remaining home was propped up with thick timber beams. All the houses that had once backed on to the sole survivor had also gone and the tarmac tide lapped round the house on three sides like the sea round a lone sandcastle on the beach. It was this house and the frightened old man who sheltered within it that were to be the centre of the morning's action; the focus of entertainment for the expectant groups from the new apartment blocks who had come to see the last of their former neighbours being evicted.

Bill Hanley walked forward to where, directly opposite the front gate of the lone house, stood the main group of officials. They were all staring at the hovel as if, now that the moment had finally come, they did not know how to go about it. There was not much to look at. Fronting the pavement was a low brick wall, separating pavement and what purported to be the front garden: no garden at all, just a few feet of tangled weeds. The front door stood to one side of the house, chipped and dented by the numerous stones that had been flung at it. Hanley knew that behind the door would be a yard-square lobby and straight ahead the narrow stairs that led up. To the right of the lobby would be the door to the single sitting room, whose broken, cardboard-stuffed windows flanked the door. Between the two was the passage running to the small, filthy kitchen and the door leading to the yard and the outside privy. The sitting room would have a tiny fire-place, for the chimney running up the side of the house still jutted to the weeping sky. Behind the house, Hanley had seen from the side view, was a back yard wide as the width of the house and twenty-five feet long. The yard was fringed by a six-foot high timber plank fence. Inside the yard, so Hanley had been told by those who had peered over the fence, the bare earth was slick with the droppings of the four speckled hens the old man kept in a hutch at the foot of the yard, up against the back fence. And that was it.

The City Council had done its best for the old man. There had been offers of re-housing in a bright, clean, new council flat; even a small house of his own somewhere else. There had been social workers, and relief workers, and church workers round to see him. They had reasoned and cajoled; given him deadline after deadline. He had refused to move. The street had come down around him and behind him and in front of him. He would not go. The work had gone on; the car park had been levelled and paved and fenced on three sides of him. Still the old man would not shift.

The local Press had had quite a field day with the "Hermit of Mayo Road". So had the local kids, who had pelted the house with rocks and mud balls, breaking most of the windows while the old man, to their intense delight, shouted obscenities at them through the shattered panes.

Finally, the City Council had issued its eviction notice, the magistrate had given permission for forcible removal of the occupant, and the might of the city had ranged itself before the front door on a wet November morning.

The Chief Housing Officer greeted Hanley.

"Unpleasant business," he said. "Always is. Hate these evictions."

"Aye," said Hanley and scanned the group. There were the two bailiffs who would do the job, big, burly men looking embarrassed. Two more from the Council, two of Hanley's own policemen, someone from Health and Welfare, a local doctor, an assortment of minor officialdom. Barney Kelleher, the veteran photographer from the local newspaper was there, with a beardless young cub reporter in tow. Hanley had good relations with the local Press and a friendly if guarded relationship with its older servants. They both had jobs to do; no need to make a guerrilla war out of it. Barney winked; Hanley nodded back. The cub took this as a sign of intimacy.

"Will you be bringing him out by force?" he asked brightly. Barney Kelleher shot him a look of venom. Hanley swivelled his grey eyes to the sprog and held the gaze until the young man wished he had not spoken.

"We will be as gentle as we can," he said gravely. The sprog scribbled furiously, more for something to do than because he could not remember such a short sentence.

The magistrate's order specified nine o'clock. It was two minutes past nine. Hanley nodded to the Chief Housing Officer.

"Proceed," he said.

The council officer approached the door of the house and knocked loudly. There was no answer.

"Are you there, Mr. Larkin?" he called. No answer. The official looked back at Hanley. Hanley nodded. Clearing his throat, the official read out the eviction order in a voice loud enough to be heard inside the house. There was no answer. He stepped back to the group in the road.

"Will we give him five minutes?" he asked.

"Very well," said Hanley. Behind the crush barrier a murmur started among the growing crowd of former dwellers in the Gloucester Diamond. Finally one at the back became bolder.

"Leave him alone," called the voice. "Poor old man."

Hanley strolled leisurely over to the barrier. Without haste he walked down the line of faces, staring into the eyes of each. Most looked away; all fell silent.

"Is it sympathy you'd be giving him?" asked Hanley softly. "Was it sympathy that broke all his windows last winter and himself freezing in there? Was it sympathy that had him pelted with stones and muck?" There was a long silence. "Hold your hour," said Hanley and walked back to the group by the front door. There was silence behind the barrier. Hanley nodded to the two bailiffs who were staring at him.

"On you go," he said.

Both men had crowbars. One walked round the side of the house, between the chain-link fence and the corner of the brickwork. With skilled ease, he prised loose three of the fence planks and entered the back yard. He walked to the back door and rapped at it with his bar. When his colleague at the front heard the sound, he rapped at the front. There was no reply to either. The man at the front inserted the tip of the crowbar between the door and side post and had it open in a trice. The door yielded three inches and stopped. There was furniture behind it. The bailiff shook his head sadly and, turning to the other edge of the door, whisked off both hinges. Then he picked up the door like a playing card and laid it in the front garden. Piece by piece, he removed the pile of chairs and tables in the hallway until the space was clear. Finally he entered the lobby, calling "Mr. Larkin?" From the back there was a splintering sound as his friend entered through the kitchen.

There was silence in the street while the men searched the ground floor. At the upper bedroom window a pale face appeared. The crowd spotted it.

"There he is," yelled three or four voices from the crowd, like hunt followers spotting the fox before the riders. Just trying to be helpful. One of the bailiffs popped his head round the front door. Hanley nodded upwards towards the bedroom window; the two men clumped up the narrow stairs. The face disappeared. There was no scuffle. In a minute they were coming down, the leader cradling a frail old man in his arms.

He emerged into the drizzle and stood undecided. The Relief worker hurried forward with a dry blanket. The bailiff set the old man down on his feet and the blanket was wrapped round him. He looked underfed and slightly dazed, but most of all, very frightened. Hanley made up his mind. He turned towards his car and beckoned the driver forward. The Council could have him later for the old folks home, but first a damn good breakfast and a hot cup of tea was called for.

"Put him in the back," he told the bailiff. When the old man was settled in the warm rear seat of the car, Hanley climbed in beside him.

"Let's get out of here," said Hanley to his driver. "There's a transport café half a mile down here and second left. We'll go there."

As the car moved back through the barrier and past the staring crowd, Hanley gave a glance at his unusual guest. The old man was dressed in grubby slacks and a thin jacket over an unbuttoned shirt. Word had it he had not looked after himself properly for years, and his face was pinched and sallow. He stared silently at the back of the car seat in front of him, not returning Hanley's gaze.

"It had to come sooner or later," said Hanley gently. "You knew that all along."

Despite his size and the capacity, when he wished to use it, to cause hard villains from the dockland to wet their knickers when he faced them, Big Bill Hanley was a much kinder man than his meaty face and twice-broken nose would give cause to think. The old man turned slowly and stared at him, but he said nothing.

"Moving house, I mean," said Hanley. "They'll fix you up a nice place, warm in winter, and decent food. You'll see."

The car drew up at the café. Hanley descended and turned to his driver.

"Bring him in," he said.

Inside the warm and steamy café, Hanley nodded to a vacant corner table. The police driver escorted the old man to the corner and sat him down, back to the wall. The old man said nothing, neither of thanks nor protestation. Hanley glanced at the wall chart behind the counter. The café owner wiped his hands on a damp dishcloth and looked enquiring.

"Double eggs, bacon, tomatoes, sausage and chips," said Hanley. "In the corner. The old fella. And start with a mug of tea." He placed two pound notes on the counter. "I'll be back for the change," he said.

The driver returned from the corner table to the counter.

"Stay there and keep an eye on him," said Hanley. "I'll be taking the car myself." The driver thought it was his lucky day; first a warm car, now a warm café. Time for a cup of tea and a smoke.

"Will I sit with him, Sir?" he asked. "He smells a bit."

"Keep an eye on him," repeated Hanley. He drove himself back to the demolition site in Mayo Road.

The team had been all ready prepared and they were not wasting time. A line of contractor's men came in and out of the house, bearing the squalid goods and chattels of the former occupant which they deposited in the road under the now streaming rain. The Council housing officer had his umbrella up and watched. Inside the car park compound two mechanical shovels on their rubber wheels waiting to begin on the rear of the house, the back yard and small privy. Behind them waiting a line of ten tipper trucks to carry away the rubble of the house. Mains water, electric current and gas had been cut off months ago; and the house was damp and filthy as a result. Sewage there had never been, hence the outside privy which had been served by a buried septic tank, soon to be filled in and concreted over for ever. The Council housing officer approached Hanley when he got out of his car again. He gestured towards the open back of a Council van.

"I've saved what we could of any sentimental value," he volunteered. "Old photos, coins, some medal ribbons, some personal clothes, a few personal documents in a cigar box, mostly mouldy. As for the furniture," — he indicated the pile of bric-a-brac in the rain — "it's alive; the Medical Officer has advised us to burn the lot. You wouldn't get tuppence for it."

"Aye," said Hanley. The official was right, but that was his problem. Still, he seemed to want moral support.

"Will he get compensation for this?" asked Hanley.

"Oh yes," said the official eagerly, anxious to explain that his Department was not a heartless beast. "For the house, which was his own title property, and a fair valuation for the furniture, fixtures, fittings and any personal effects lost, damaged or destroyed. And a displacement allowance to cover the inconvenience of moving — though frankly he's cost the Council a lot more than the total by refusing to quit for so long."

At this moment, one of the men came from round the side of the house carrying two chickens, head down, in each hand.

"What the hell do I do with these?" he asked no one in particular. One of his colleagues told him. Barney Kelleher snapped off a photo. Good picture, that, he thought. The last friends of the Hermit of Mayo Road. Nice caption. One of the contractor's men said he too kept chickens and could put them in with his small flock. A cardboard carton was found, the damp birds popped inside and they went in the Council van until they could go to the workman's home.

Within an hour, it was over. The small house was gutted. A burly foreman in gleaming yellow oilskins came over to the Council official.

"Can we start?" he asked. "The boss wants the car park finished and fenced. If we can concrete by tonight, we can tar it over tomorrow first thing."

The official sighed. "Go ahead," he said. The foreman turned and waved toward a mobile crane from whose arm swung a half-ton iron ball. Gently the crane moved forward to the flank of the house, planted itself and rose with a soft hiss onto its hydraulic feet. The ball began to swing, gently at first, then in bigger arcs. The crowd watched fascinated. They had seen their own houses go down in just this way, but it never palled. Finally, the ball thumped into the side of the house, not far from the chimney, splintering a dozen bricks and sending two cracks racing down the wall. The crowd gave a long, low, "Aaaaaah". There's nothing like a nice bit of demolition to cheer up a bored crowd. At the fourth crunch, two upper windows popped out from their frames and fell into the car park. A corner of the house detached itself from the rest, waltzed slowly in a half spiral and collapsed into the back yard. Moments later, the chimney stack, a solid column of brick, snapped at the mid-section and the upper portion crashed through the roof and down through the floor to ground level. The old house was coming apart. The crowd loved it. Chief Superintendent Hanley got back into his car and returned to the café.

It was even warmer and steamier than before. His driver sat at the bar counter before a steaming cup of tea. He stubbed out a cigarette as Hanley walked in and slithered from his bar stool. The old man seemed busy in the corner.

"Is he finished yet?" asked Hanley.

"He's taking a powerful long time, sir," said the driver. "And the buttered bread is going down like there was no tomorrow."

Hanley watched as the old man embalmed yet another morsel of greasy fried food in soft, white bread and began to chew.

"The bread'll be extra," said the café owner. "He's had three portions already."

Hanley glanced at his watch. It was past eleven. He sighed and hoisted himself on a stool.

"A mug of tea," he said. He had told the Health and Welfare official to join him in thirty minutes and take the old man into Council care. Then he could get back to his office and on with some paper work. He'd be glad to be shot of the whole business.

Barney Kelleher and his cub reporter came in.

"Buying him breakfast, are you?" asked Barney.

"I'll claim it back," said Hanley. Kelleher knew he wouldn't. "Get some pictures?" Barney shrugged.

"Not bad," he said. "Nice one of the chickens. And the chimney stack coming down. And himself being brought out in a blanket. End of an era. I remember the days when ten thousand people lived in the Diamond. And all of them at work. Poor paid, mind you, but working. It took fifty years to create a slum in those days. Now they can do it in five."

Hanley grunted. "That's progress," he said.

A second police car drew up at the door. One of the young officers who had been at Mayo Road jumped out, saw through the glass that his chief was with the Press and halted irresolute. The cub reporter did not notice. Barney Kelleher pretended not to. Hanley slid off his stool and went to the door. Outside in the rain the policeman told him, "You'd better come back, sir. They've . . . found something."

Hanley beckoned to his driver who came out to the pavement. "I'm going back," said Hanley. "Keep an eye on the old man." He glanced back into the café.

At the far back the old man had stopped eating. He held a fork in one hand, a piece of rolled bread containing half a sausage in the other, perfectly immobile, as he stared silently at the three uniforms on the pavement.

Back at the site, all work had stopped. The demolition men in their oilskins and hard hats stood grouped in a circle in the rubble of the building. The remaining policeman was with them. Hanley strode from his car, picking his way over the shattered piles of brick, to where the circle of men stared downwards. From behind him the remnants of the crowd murmured. "It's the old man's treasure," whispered someone loudly from the crowd. There was a murmur of agreement. "He had a fortune buried there; that's why he'd never leave."

Hanley arrived at the centre of the group and looked at the area of attention. The short stump of the shattered chimney stack still stood, five feet high, surrounded by piles of debris. At the base of the stack, the old black fireplace could still be seen. To one side a couple of feet of outer house-wall still stood. At its base, inside the house was a collection of fallen bricks, from which protruded the shrunken and wizened, but still recognisable leg of a human being. A shred of what looked like nylon stocking still clung below the kneecap.

"Who found it?" asked Hanley. The foreman stepped forward.

"Tommy here was working on the chimney breast with a pick. He cleared some bricks to get a better swing. He saw it. He called me." Hanley recognised a good witness when he saw one.

"Was it under the floorboards, then?" asked Hanley.

"No. This whole area was built on a marsh. The builders cemented in the floors."

"Where was it then?"

The foreman leaned down and pointed to the stump of the fireplace. "From the inside of the sitting room the fireplace looked to be flush with the wall. In fact it wasn't. Originally it jutted out from the house wall. Someone ran up a quick brick wall between the chimney breast and the end of the room, forming a cavity twelve inches deep, right up to the room ceiling. And another on the other side of the fireplace to give symmetry. But the other one was empty. The body was in the cavity between the false wall and the house-wall. Even the room was re-papered to cover the work. See, the same paper on the front of the chimney breast as on the false wall."

Hanley followed his finger; shreds of the same damp-mottled wallpaper adhered to the front of the chimney breast above the mantel-shelf and to the bricks surrounding and part-covering the body. It was an old paper with a rosebud pattern on it. But on the inside of the original house-wall beside the fireplace, a dingy and even older striped wallpaper could be discerned. Hanley stood up.

"Right," he said. "That's the end of your work for today. You might as well stand the men down and let them go. We'll be taking over from here." The hard hats began to move back off the pile of bricks. Hanley turned to his two policemen.

"Keep the crowd barriers up," he said. "The whole place sealed off. More men will be coming, and more barriers. I want this place unapproached from any of the four sides. I'll get more manpower up here and the forensic boys. Nothing touched until they say so, okay?"

The two men saluted. Hanley heaved himself back into his car and called precinct headquarters. He issued a stream of orders, then had himself patched through to the Technical Section of the Investigation Bureau, tucked away in a grim old Victorian barracks behind Heuston Railway Station. He was lucky. Detective Superintendent O'Keeffe came on the line, and they had known each other many years. Hanley told him what had been found and what he needed.

"I'll get them up there," O'Keefe's voice crackled down the line. "Do you want the Murder Squad brought in?"

Hanley sniffed. "No thanks. I think we can handle this one at Divisional level."

"Do you have a suspect then?" asked O'Keefe.

"Oh, yes, we have one of those all right," said Hanley.

He drove himself back to the café, passing Barney Kelleher who was trying unsuccessfully to get back through the crowd barrier. This time, the patrolman on duty was not being nearly so helpful.

At the café, Hanley found his driver still at the counter with another cup of tea. At the rear sat the old man, meal finished, sipping a cup of tea. He stared at Hanley as the giant policeman came over to him.

"We've found her," said Hanley, leaning over the table and speaking so softly that no one else in the room could hear him. "We'd better be going, had we not, Mr. Larkin? Down to the station, now? We have to do a little talking, do we not?"

The old man stared back without a word. It occurred to Hanley that so far he had not opened his mouth to say a word. Something flickered in the old man's eyes. Fear? Relief? Probably fear. No wonder he had been afraid all these years.

He rose quietly and with Hanley's firm hand on his elbow went out to the police car. The driver followed and climbed behind the wheel. The rain had stopped and a chill wind blew toffee papers like autumn leaves down the street where no trees grew. The car drew away from the kerb. The old man sat hunched, staring ahead, silent.

"Back to the station," said Hanley.

There is no country in the world where a murder investigation is a matter of inspired guesses as television would have it. They are ninety per cent plodding routine, formalities to be gone through, procedures to be fulfilled. And administration, plenty of that.

Big Bill Hanley saw the old man settled into a cell at the back of the charge room; he made no protest, asked for no lawyer. Hanley had no intention of charging him — yet. He could hold him on suspicion for at lease twenty-four hours and he wanted more facts first. Then he sat at his desk and started with the telephone.

"By the book, lad, by the book. We're not Sherlock Holmes," his old sergeant used to tell him, years before. Good advice. More cases have been lost in court by procedural screw-ups than have ever been won by intellectual brilliance.

Hanley formally informed the City Coroner of the fact of a death, catching the senior civil servant just as he was leaving for his lunch. Then he told the City Morgue in Store Street, just behind the bus terminal, that there would be a complex post mortem that afternoon. He traced the State Pathologist, Professor Tim McCarthy, who listened calmly on a telephone in the hallway of the Kildare Club, sighed at the thought of missing the excellent breast of pheasant that was on the menu, and agreed to come at once.

There were canvas screens to be organised, and men detailed to pick up picks and shovels and report to Mayo Road. He summoned the three detectives attached to his precinct from their lunch in the canteen to his office, and made do with two sandwiches and a pint of milk as he worked.

"I know you are busy," he told them. "We all are. That's why I want this one tied up fast. It shouldn't take too long."

He named his Detective Chief Inspector to be scene-of-crime examiner and despatched him to Mayo Road without delay. The two young sergeants got separate jobs. One was detailed to check into the house itself; the council official had said the old man owned it, freehold, but the Rating Office at the City Hall would have details of its past history and ownership. The Registry of Deeds would clinch the final details.

The second detective sergeant got the leg-work; trace every former occupant of Mayo Road, most of them now re-housed in the council apartment blocks. Find the neighbours, the gossips, the shopkeepers, the patrolmen who had had the beat including Mayo Road for the past fifteen years before its demolition, the local priest — anybody who had known Mayo Road and the old man for as many years back as possible. And that, said Hanley with emphasis, includes anyone who ever knew Mrs., that is, the late Mrs. Larkin.

He despatched a uniformed sergeant with a van to repossess all the personal memorabilia from the destroyed house that he had seen in the council van that morning, and to bring all the abandoned furniture, fleas and all, into the police station yard.

It was past two in the afternoon when he finally rose and stretched. He instructed that the old man be brought to the interview room, finished his milk and waited five minutes. When he walked into the interview room, the old man was seated at the table, hands clasped in front of him, staring at the wall. A policeman stood near the door.

"Any word from him?" murmured Hanley to the officer.

"No, sir. Not a thing." Hanley nodded for him to go.

When they were alone, he sat at the table facing the old man. Herbert James Larkin, the Council records showed.

"Well, now, Mr. Larkin," said Hanley softly. "Don't you think it would be a sensible thing to tell me about it?"

His experience told him there was no use trying to bully the old man. This was no street villain from the underworld. He'd had three wife murderers in his time, and all of them mild, meek little fellows who had soon seemed relieved to get rid of the awful details to the big sympathetic man across the table. The old man slowly looked up at him, held his gaze for a few moments, and looked back at the table. Hanley took out a packet of cigarettes and flipped it open.

"Smoke?" he said. The old man didn't move. "Actually I don't use them myself either," said Hanley, but he left the pack invitingly open on the table, a box of matches beside it.

"Not a bad try," he conceded. "Holding on to the house like that, all those months. But the Council had to win sooner or later. You knew that, didn't you? Must have been awful, knowing that they'd send the bailiffs for you sooner or later."

He waited for a comment, any hint of communication from the old man. There was none. No matter, he was patient as an ox when he wanted a man to talk. And they all talked sooner or later. It was the relief really. The unburdening. The Church knew all about the relief of confession.

"How many years, Mr. Larkin? How many years of anxiety, of waiting? How many months since the first bulldozers moved into the area, eh? Man, what you must have gone through."

The old man lifted his gaze and met Hanley's eyes, maybe searching for something, a fellow human being after years of self-imposed isolation; a little sympathy perhaps. Hanley felt he was nearly there. The old man's eyes swivelled away, over Hanley's shoulder to the rear wall.

"It's over, Mr. Larkin. All over. It's got to come out, sooner or later. We'll go back through the years, slowly, plodding away, and we'll piece it together. You know that. It was Mrs. Larkin, wasn't it? Why? Another man? Or just an argument?

Maybe it was just an accident, eh? So you panicked, and then you were committed; to living like a hermit all your days."

The old man's lower lip moved. He ran his tongue along it. I'm getting through, thought Hanley. Not long now.

"It must have been bad, these past years," he went on. "Sitting there all alone, no friends like before it happened, just you and the knowledge that she was still there, not far away, bricked away beside the fireplace."

Something flickered in the old man's eyes. Shock at the memory? Perhaps the shock treatment would work better. He blinked twice. I'm nearly there, thought Hanley, I'm nearly there. But when the old man's eyes moved back to meet his own, they were blank again. He said nothing.

Hanley kept it up for another hour, but the old man never uttered a word.

"Please yourself," said Hanley as he rose. "I'll be back, and we'll talk it over then."

When he arrived at Mayo Road, the scene was a hive of activity, the crowd bigger than before, but able to see far less. On all four sides, the ruin of the house was surrounded by canvas screens, whipped by the wind, but enough to keep prying eyes from seeing the job going on within. Inside the hollow square that included a portion of the roadway, twenty hefty policemen in heavy boots and rummage gear were pulling the rubble to pieces by hand. Each brick and slate, each shattered timber from the stairs and banisters, each tile and ceiling joist, was carefully plucked out, examined for whatever it might show, which was nothing, and tossed out into the roadway, where the rubble mounted higher and higher. The contents of cupboards were examined, the cupboards themselves ripped out to see if there was anything behind them. All walls were tapped to see if they contained hollow cavities before they were pulled down brick by brick and thrown into the road.

Round the fireplace, two men worked with special care. The rubble on top of the corpse was lifted carefully away until only a thick film of dust covered the body. It was bent into an embryo posture, lying on its side, though in its cavity it had probably sat upright, facing sideways. Professor McCarthy, looking over what was left of the house wall, directed these two men at their work. When it was done to his satisfaction, he entered the cavity among the remaining bricks and with a soft brush, like a careful housewife, began to whisk away the creamy dust of the old mortar.

When he had cleared the majority of the dust, he examined the body more closely, tapped part of the exposed thigh and of the upper arm, and emerged from the cavity.

"It's a mummy," he told Hanley.

"A mummy?"

"Just so. With a brick or concrete floor, a sealed environment on all six sides, and the warmth of the fireplace two feet away, mummification has taken place. Dehydration, but with preservation. The organs may well be intact, but hard as wood. No use trying to cut tonight. I'll need the warm glycerine bath. It'll take time."

"How long?" asked Hanley.

"Twelve hours at least. Maybe more. I've known it take days." The Professor glanced at his watch. "It's nearly four. I'll have it immersed by five. Tomorrow morning around nine, I'll look in at the morgue and see if I can start."

"Blast," said Hanley. "I wanted this one sewn up."

"An unfortunate choice of words," said McCarthy. "I'll do the best I can. Actually, I don't think the organs will tell us much. From what I can see there's a ligature round the neck."

"Strangulation, eh?"

"Maybe," said McCarthy. The undertaker who always got the City contracts had his van parked out beyond the screens. Under the State Pathologist's supervision, two of his men lifted the rigid corpse, still on its side, onto a bier, covered it with a large blanket and transferred their cargo to the waiting hearse. Followed by the Professor, they sped off to Store Street and the City Morgue. Hanley walked over to the fingerprint man from Tech. Bureau.

"Anything here for you?" he asked. The man shrugged.

"It's all brick and rubble in there, sir. There's not a clean surface in the place."

"How about you?" Hanley asked the photographer from the same office.

"I'll need a bit more, sir. I'll wait until the boys have got it cleared down to the floor, then see if there's anything there. If not, I've got it for tonight."

The gang foreman from the contractor wandered over. He had been kept standing by at Hanley's suggestion, as a technical expert in case of hazard from falling rubble. He grinned.

"That's a lovely job you've done there," he said in his broad Dublin accent. "There'll not be much for my lads left to do."

Hanley gestured to the street where most of the house now lay in a single large mound of brick and timber debris.

"You can start shifting that if you like. We're finished with it," he said. The foreman glanced at his watch in the gathering gloom.

"There's an hour left," he said. "We'll get most of it shifted. Can we start on the rest of the house tomorrow? The boss wants to get that park finished and fenced."

"Check with me at nine tomorrow morning. I'll let you know," he said. Before leaving he called over his Detective Chief Inspector who had been organising it all.

"There are portable lights coming," he said. "Have the lads bring it down to floor level and search the floor surface for any signs of interference since it was laid down."

The detective nodded. "So far it's just the one hiding place," he said. "But I'll keep looking till it's clean."

Back at the station, Hanley got the first chance to look at something that might tell him about the old man in the cells. On his desk was the pile of assorted odds and ends that the bailiffs had removed from the house that morning and put into the council van. He went through each document carefully, using a magnifying glass to read the old and faded lettering.

There was a birth certificate, giving the name of the old man, his place of birth as Dublin and his age. He was 67, having been born in 1911. There were some old letters, but from people who meant nothing to Hanley, mostly from long ago, and their contents had no seeming bearing on the case. But two things were of interest. One was a faded photograph, mottled and warped, in a cheap frame, but unglassed. It showed a soldier in what looked like British Army uniform, smiling uncertainly into the camera. Hanley recognised a much younger version of the old man in the cells. On his arm was a plump young woman with a posy of flowers; no wedding dress but a neutral coloured two-piece suit with the high-square shoulders of the mid to late 1940s.

The other item was the cigar-box. It contained more letters, also irrelevant to the case, three medal ribbons clipped to a bar with a pin behind it, and a British Army service pay-book. Hanley reached for the telephone. It was twenty past five, but he might be lucky. He was. The Military Attaché at the British Embassy out at Sandyford was still at his desk. Hanley explained his problem. Major Dawkins said he would be glad to help if he could, unofficially, of course. Of course. Official requests have to go through channels. Officially all contact between the Irish police force and Britain goes through channels. Unofficially, contacts are much closer than either side would be prepared to concede to the idle enquirer. Major Dawkins agreed to stop by the police station on his way home, even though it meant quite a detour.

Darkness had long fallen when the first of the two young detectives doing the leg work reported back. The first was the man who had been checking the register of deeds and the rating lists. Seated in front of Hanley's desk, he flicked open his notebook and recited.

The house at 38 Mayo Road had been bought, so the records of deeds showed, by Herbert James Larkin in 1954 from the estate of the previous owner, then deceased. He had paid £400 for the property, title freehold. No evidence of a mortgage, so he had had the money available. The rating list showed the house to have been owned since that date by the same Herbert James Larkin and occupied by Mr. Herbert James Larkin and Mrs. Violet Larkin. No record of the wife's decease or departure, but then the rating list would not show a change of occupancy, even in part, unless advised in writing by the continuing occupant, which had not happened. But a search of the death certificates over at the Custom House, going back to 1954, revealed no trace of the death of any Mrs. Violet Larkin, of that address or any other.

Department of Health and Welfare records showed Larkin drew a state pension for the past two years, never applied for supplementary benefit, and prior to pensionable retirement was apparently a store-keeper and nightwatchman. One last thing, said the sergeant. His internal PAYE forms, starting in 1954, had shown a previous address in North London, England.

Hanley flicked the Army pay-book across the desk.

"So he was in the British Army," said the sergeant.

"Nothing strange in that," said Hanley. "There were fifty thousand Irishmen in the British Armed Forces during the Second World War. Larkin was one of them, it seems."

"Perhaps the wife was English. He came back to Dublin in 1954 with her from North London."

"Likely she was," said Hanley, pushing over the wedding photo. "He married her in uniform."

The internal phone rang to inform him the Military Attaché from the British Embassy was at the front desk. Hanley nodded at his sergeant, who left. "Show him in, please," said Hanley.

Major Dawkins was Hanley's luckiest find of the day. He crossed his pin-stripe-clad legs elegantly, aimed a glittering toe cap at Hanley across the desk and listened quietly. Then he studied the wedding photograph intently for a while.

Finally he came round the desk and stood by Hanley's shoulder with the magnifying glass in one hand and his gold propelling pencil in the other. With the tip of the pencil, he tapped the cap badge above Larkin's face in the photograph.

"King's Dragoon Guards," he said with certainty.

"How do you know that?" asked Hanley.

Major Dawkins passed Hanley the magnifying glass.

"The double-headed eagle," he said. "Cap badge of the King's Dragoon Guards. Very distinctive. None like it."

"Anything else," asked Hanley.

Dawkins pointed to the three medals on the chest of the newly-wed.

"This first one is the 1939-1945 Star," he said, "and the third one at the end is the Victory Medal. But the one in the middle is the Africa Star with what looks like the bar-clasp of the Eighth Army across it. That makes sense. The King's Dragoon Guards fought againt Rommel in North Africa. Armoured cars, actually."

Hanley brought out the three medal ribbons. Those in the

photograph were the full ceremonial medals; those on the desk were the smaller version — the miniatures on a bar — for wearing with un-dress uniform.

"Ah, yes," said Major Dawkins, with a glance at them. "The same pattern, see. And the Eighth Army bar."

With the glass, Hanley could make out that the pattern was the same. He passed Major Dawkins the service pay-book. Dawkins' eyes lit up. He flicked through the pages.

"Volunteered at Liverpool, October 1940," he said, "probably at Burton's."

"Burton's?" asked Hanley.

"Burton, the tailors. It was the recruiting centre at Liverpool during the war. A lot of the Irish volunteers arrived at Liverpool docks and were directed there by the recruiting sergeants. Demobilised January 1946. Honourable discharge. Odd."

"What?" asked Hanley.

"Volunteered in 1940. Fought in action with armoured cars in North Africa. Stayed until 1946. But he stayed a Trooper. Never won a stripe on his arm. Never made corporal." He tapped the uniformed arm in the wedding photograph.

"Perhaps he was a bad soldier," suggested Hanley.

"Possibly."

"Can you get me some more details of his war record?" asked Hanley.

"First thing in the morning," said Dawkins. He noted most of the details in the pay-book and left.

Hanley had a canteen supper and waited for his second detective sergeant to report back. The man arrived at well past ten-thirty, tired but triumphant.

"I spoke with fifteen of those who knew Larkin and his wife in Mayo Road," he said, "and three came up trumps. Mrs. Moran, the next-door neighbour. She's been there for thirty years and remembers the Larkins moving in. The postman, now retired, who served Mayo Road up till last year, and Father Byrne, also retired, now living in a priests' retired home out at Inchicore. I've just got back from there, hence the delay."

Hanley sat back as the detective flicked back to the start of his notebook and began to report.

"Mrs. Moran recalled that in 1954 the widower who had lived there, at Number 38, died and shortly afterwards, a 'For Sale' notice went up on the house. It was only there a fortnight, then it came down. A fortnight later, the Larkins moved in. Larkin was then about 45, his wife much younger. She was English, a Londoner, and told Mrs. Moran they had moved from London where her husband had been a store clerk. One summer, Mrs. Larkin disappeared; Mrs. Moran put the year at 1963."

"How is she so certain?" asked Hanley.

"That November Kennedy was killed," said the detective sergeant. "The news came from the lounge bar up the street where there was a television set. Within twenty minutes everyone in Mayo Road was on the pavement discussing it. Mrs. Moran was so excited she burst into Larkin's house next door to tell him. She didn't knock, just walked into the sitting room. Larkin was dozing in a chair. He jumped up in great alarm and couldn't wait to get her out of the house. Mrs. Larkin had left by then. But she was there in the spring and summer; she used to baby-sit for the Morans on a Saturday night; Mrs. Moran's second baby was born in January 1963. So it was the late summer of sixty-three that Mrs. Larkin disappeared."

"What was the reason given?" asked Hanley.

"Walked out on him," said the detective without hesitation. "No one doubted it. He worked hard, but never wanted to go out in the evening, not even Saturday, hence Mrs. Larkin's availability as a baby-sitter. There were rows about it. Something else; she was flighty, a bit of a flirt. When she packed her bags and left him, no one was surprised. Some of the women reckoned he deserved it for not treating her better. No one suspected anything."

"After that, Larkin kept himself even more to himself. Hardly ever went out, ceased to care much for himself or the house. People offered to help out, as they do in small communities, but he rejected all offers. Eventually people left him alone. A couple of years later, he lost his job as a storeman and became a nightwatchman, leaving after dark and returning at sunrise. Kept the door bolted on the inside, at night because he was out, by day because he wanted to sleep. So he said. He also started keeping pets. First ferrets, in a shed in the back garden. But they escaped. Then pigeons, but they flew off or were shot elsewhere. Finally chickens, for the past ten years."

The parish priest confirmed much of Mrs. Moran's recollections. Mrs. Larkin had been English, but a Catholic and a church-goer. She had confessed regularly. Then in August 1963 she had gone off, most people said with a man friend, and Father Byrne had had no reason to doubt. He would not break the confessional oath, but he would go as far as to say he did not doubt it. He had called at the house several times, but Larkin was not a church-goer and refused all spiritual comfort. He had called his departed wife a tart.

"It all fits," mused Hanley. "She could well have been about to leave him when he found out and thumped her a bit too hard. God knows, it's happened enough times."

The postman had little more to add. He was a local man and used the local bar. Mrs. Larkin had liked to have her noggin on a Saturday night, had even helped out as a barmaid one summer, but her husband soon put a stop to that. He recalled she was much younger than Larkin, bright and bubbly, not averse to a bit of flirting.

"Description?" asked Hanley.

"She was short, about five feet, three inches. Rather plump, well-rounded anyway. Curling dark hair. Giggled a lot. Plenty of chest. Postman recalled when she pulled a pint of ale from those old style beer pumps they used to have, it was worth watching. But Larkin went wild when he found out. Came in and pulled her home. She left him, or disappeared, soon afterwards."

Hanley rose and stretched. It was nearly midnight. He clapped a hand on the young detective's shoulder.

"It's late. Get yourself home. Write it all up in the morning."

Hanley's last visitor of the night was his Chief Inspector, the scene-of-crime investigator.

"It's clean," he told Hanley. "The last brick removed, and not a sign of anything else that might be helpful."

"Then it's up to the poor woman's body to tell us the rest of what we want to know," said Hanley. "Or Larkin himself."

"Has he talked yet?" asked the Chief Inspector.

"Not yet," said Hanley, "but he will. They all talk in the end."

The Chief Inspector went home. Hanley called his wife and told her he would be spending the night at the station. Just after midnight, he went down to the cells. The old man was awake, sitting on the edge of his bunk, staring at the opposite wall. Hanley jerked his head at the police officer with him and they all trooped up to the interview room. The policeman sat in a corner with his notebook at the ready. Hanley faced the old man and read him the caution:

"Herbert James Larkin, you are not obliged to say anything. But anything you say will be taken down and may be used in evidence."

Then he sat down opposite the old man.

"Fifteen years, Mr. Larkin. That's a long time to live with a thing like that. August of 1963, wasn't it? The neighbours remember it; the priest remembers it; even the postman remembers it. Now, why don't you tell me about it?"

The old man raised his eyes, held Hanley's gaze for a few seconds, then lowered his eyes to the table. He said nothing. Hanley kept it up almost until dawn. Larkin seemed not to tire, although the policeman in the corner yawned repeatedly. Larkin had been a nightwatchman for years, Hanley recalled. Probably more awake at night now than during the day.

There was a grey light filtering through the frosted-glass window of the interview room when he rose finally.

"Have it your own way," he said. "You may not talk, but your Violet will. Strange that, eh? Talking back from the grave behind the wall, fifteen years later. But she'll talk to the State Pathologist, in a few hours now. She'll talk. She'll tell him in his laboratory what happened to her, when it happened, maybe even why it happened. Then we'll come here again, and I'll charge you."

Slow to anger though he was, he was becoming irritated by the silence of the old man. It was not that he said little; he said absolutely nothing. Just stared back at Hanley with that strange look in his eyes. What *was* that look, Hanley asked himself. Trepidation? Fear of him, Hanley? Remorse? Relief? Murderers were often relieved, but then they usually spoke. Mockery? No, not mockery. The man's number was up.

Finally he rose, rubbed a large hand round the stubble on his chin and went back to his office. Larkin went back to the cell.

Hanley snatched three hours sleep in his chair, head tilted back, feet out, snoring loudly. At eight he rose, went to the rest room and washed and shaved. Two startled young police cadets surprised him there at half-past eight as they came on duty and went about their business like two dormice in carpet slippers. At nine he was breakfasted and working his way through a mountain of accumulated paper-work. At nine-thirty, the contractor's foreman at the Mayo Road job came on the line. Hanley considered his request.

"All right," he said at last, "you can fence it in and concrete over."

Twenty minutes later, Professor McCarthy was on the line.

"I've got the limbs straightened out," he said cheerfully. "And the skin is soft enough to take the scalpel. We're draining and drying it off now. I'll begin in an hour."

"When can you give me a report?" asked Hanley.

"Depends what you mean," came the voice down the line. "The official report will take two to three days. Unofficially, I should have something just after lunch. Cause of death at least. We've confirmed the ligature round the neck. It was a nylon stocking, as I suspected yesterday."

The Pathologist agreed to come the mile from the Store Street Morgue to Hanley's office by two-thirty.

The morning was uninterrupted, save by Major Dawkins, who phoned at midday.

"Bit of luck," he said. "Found an old friend of mine in the Records Office at the War House. He gave me priority."

"Thank you, Major," said Hanley. "I'm taking notes; go ahead."

"There's not too much, but it confirms what we thought yesterday."

What *you* thought yesterday, Hanley said to himself. This laborious English courtesy.

"Trooper Herbert James Larkin arrived on the Dublin ferry at Liverpool, October 1940 and volunteered for the Army. Basic training at Catterick Camp, Yorkshire. Transferred to the King's Dragoon Guards. Sent by troopship to join the regiment in Egypt in March 1941. Then we come to the reason he never made corporal."

"Which was?"

"He was captured. Taken prisoner by the Germans in Rommel's autumn offensive of that year. Spent the rest of the war as a farm worker at a POW camp in Silesia, eastern end of the Third Reich. Liberated by the Russians, October 1944. Repatriated April 1945, just in time for the end of the war in Europe in May."

"Anything about his marriage?" asked Hanley.

"Certainly," said Major Dawkins. "He was married while a serving soldier, so the Army has that on file, too. Married at St. Mary Saviour's Catholic Church, Edmonton, North London, 14th of November, 1945. Bride, Violet Mary Smith, hotel chamber-maid. She was seventeen at the time. As you know, he got an honourable discharge in January 1946 and stayed on in Edmonton working as a storekeeper until 1954. That's when the Army has its last address for him."

Hanley thanked Dawkins profusely and hung up. Larkin was 34, turning 35, when he married a young girl of 17. She would have been a lively 26 when they came to live in Mayo Road, and he a perhaps not so lively 43. By the time she died in August 1963, she would have been a still attractive and possibly sexy 35, while he would have been a perhaps very uninteresting and uninterested 52. Yes, that might have caused problems. He waited with impatience for the visit of Professor McCarthy.

The State Pathologist was as good as his word and was seated in the chair facing Hanley by two-thirty. He took out his pipe and began leisurely to fill it.

"Can't smoke in the lab," he apologised. "Anyway, the smoke covers the formaldehyde. You should appreciate it."

He puffed contentedly.

"Got what you wanted," said Professor McCarthy easily. "Murder beyond a doubt. Manual strangulation with the use of a nylon stocking, causing asphyxiation; coupled with shock. The hyoid bone here" — pointing to the area between chin and Adam's apple — "was fractured in three places. Prior to death, a blow to the head was administered, causing scalp laceration, but not death. Probably enough to stun the victim and permit the strangulation to take place."

Hanley leaned back. "Marvellous," he said. "Anything on year of death?"

"Ah," said the Professor, reaching for his attaché case. "I have a little present for you." He reached into the case and produced a polythene bag containing what appeared to be a six-inch by four-inch fragment of yellowed and faded newspaper.

"The scalp wound must have bled a bit. To prevent a mess on the carpet, our murderer must have wrapped the area of the scalp wound in newspaper. While he built his oubliette behind the false wall, no doubt. By good fortune it's recognisable as a piece of a daily newspaper, with the date still discernible on it."

Hanley took the polythene bag and through the transparent material, with the aid of his reading spotlight, and magnifying glass, studied the newsprint fragment. Then he sat up sharply.

"Of course, this was an old piece of newspaper," he said.

"Of course it's old," said McCarthy.

"It was an old piece, a back number, when it was used to wrap the wound in the head," insisted Hanley.

McCarthy shrugged.

"You could be right," he agreed. "With this kind of mummy, one can't be accurate as to the exact year of death. But reasonably so."

Hanley relaxed.

"That's what I meant," he said with relief. "Larkin must have grabbed the newspaper lining a drawer, or a cupboard, that had been there for years untouched. That's why the date on the paper goes back to March 13th, 1943."

"So does the corpse," said McCarthy. "I put death at between 1941 and 1945. Probably within a few weeks of the date of that piece of newspaper."

Hanley started at him, long and hard.

"Mrs. Violet Mary Larkin died during August 1963," he said.

McCarthy stared at him and held the stare while he re-lit his pipe.

"I think," he said gently, "we're talking at cross-purposes."

"I'm talking about the body in the morgue," said Hanley.

"So am I," said McCarthy.

"Larkin and his wife arrived from London in 1954," said Hanley slowly. "They bought Number 38, Mayo Road, following the death of the previous owner/occupant. Mrs. Larkin was announced as having run away and left her husband in August 1963. Yesterday, we found her body bricked up behind a false wall while the house was being demolished."

"You didn't tell me how long the Larkins had been at that house," McCarthy pointed out reasonably. "You asked me to do a pathological examination of a virtually mummified body. Which I have done."

"But it *was* mummified," insisted Hanley. "Surely in those conditions there could be a wide range in the possible year of death?"

"Not twenty years," said McCarthy equably. "There is no way that body was alive after 1945. The tests on the internal organs are beyond much doubt. The nylon stockings can be analysed, of course. And the newsprint. But as you say, both could have been twenty years old at the time of use. But the hair, the nails, the organs — they couldn't."

Hanley felt as though he was living, while awake, his only nightmare. He was bulldozing his way towards the goal-line, using his strength to cut a path through the English defenders during that last Triple Crown final match in 1951. He was almost there, and the ball began slipping from his hands. Try as he might, he could not hold on to it . . . .

He recovered himself.

"Age apart, what else?" he asked. "The woman was short, about five feet, three inches?"

McCarthy shook his head. "Sorry, bones don't alter in length, even after thirty-five years behind a brick wall. She was five feet ten to eleven inches tall, bony and angular."

"Black hair, curly?" asked Hanley.

"Dead straight and ginger in colour. It's still attached to the head."

"She was about 35 at the age of death?"

"No," said McCarthy, "she was well over fifty and she had had children, two I'd say, and there had been remedial surgery done, following the second."

"Do you mean to say," asked Hanley, "that from 1954, they — until Violet Larkin walked out, and Larkin alone for the past fifteen years — have been sitting in their living room six feet from a walled-up corpse?"

"Must have done," said McCarthy. "A body in a state of mummification, which itself would occur within a short time in such a warm environment, would emit no odour. By 1954, assuming she was killed, as I think, in 1943, the body would long since have achieved exactly the same state as that in which we found her yesterday. Incidentally, where was your man Larkin in 1943?"

"In a Prisoner-of-War Camp in Silesia," said Hanley.

"Then," said the Professor, rising, "he did not kill that woman and brick her up beside the fireplace. So who did?"

Hanley picked up the internal phone and called the detectives' room. The young sergeant came on the line.

"Who," asked Hanley with deliberation, "was the man who owned and occupied the house in Mayo Road prior to 1954 and died in that year?"

"I don't know, sir," said the young man.

"How long had he been in it?"

"I didn't take notes about that, sir. But I recall the previous occupant had been there for thirty years. He was a widower."

"He certainly was," growled Hanley. "What was his name?"

There was a pause.

"I never thought to ask, sir."

The old man was released two hours later, through the back door in case of anyone from the Press hanging around the front lobby. This time, there was no police car, no escort. He had the address of a Council hostel in his pocket. Without saying a word, he shuffled off down the pavement and into the mean streets of the Diamond.

At Mayo Road, the missing section of chain-link fence where the house had once been, was in place, closing off the entire car-park. Within the area, on the spot where the house and garden had stood, was a sheet of level concrete in the last stages of drying. In the gathering dusk, the foreman was stomping over the concrete with two of his workers.

Every now and then he hacked at the surface with the steel-capped heel of one of his boots.

"Sure it's dry enough," he said. "The boss wants it finished and tarmacked over by tonight."

On the other side of the road, in the rubble field, a bonfire burned up the last of a pile of banisters, stairs, roof joists, ceiling beams, cupboards, window frames and doors, the remnants of the plank fence, the old privy and the chicken house. Even by its light, none of the workers noticed the old figure that stared at them through the chain-link wire.

The foreman finished prowling over the rectangle of new concrete and came to the far end of the plot, up against where the old back fence had been. He looked down at his feet.

"What's this?" he asked. "This isn't new. This is old."

The area he was pointing at was a slab of concrete about six feet by two.

"It was the floor of the old chicken-house," said the worker who had spread the ready-mix concrete that morning by hand.

"Did you not put a fresh layer over it?" asked the foreman.

"I did not. It would have raised the level too high at that spot. There'd have been a fierce hump in the tarmac if I had."

"If there's any subsidence here, the boss'll have us do it again, and pay for it," said the foreman darkly. He went a few feet away and came back with a heavy pointed steel bar. Raising it high above his head, he brought it down, point first, on the old concrete slab. The bar bounced back. The foreman grunted.

"All right, it's solid enough," he conceded. Turning towards the waiting bulldozer, he beckoned. "Fill it in, Michael."

The bulldozer blade came down right behind the pile of steaming fresh tarmac and began to push the hot mountain, crumbling like soft, damp sugar, towards the rectangle of concrete. Within minutes, the area had turned from grey to black, the tar raked flat and even, before the mechanical roller, waiting behind the spreaders, finished the job. As the last light faded from the sky, the man left for home and the car-park was at last complete.

Beyond the wire, the old man turned and shuffled away. He said nothing, nothing at all. But for the first time, he smiled, a long, happy smile of pure relief.

ANNE McCAFFREY

Habit Is An Old Horse

As the sussex cock summoned morning, the old grey horse woke. He lifted his muzzle from the ground and, blinking to clear his eyes, gazed about the twelve acre field. The donkeys were, as usual, already grazing at the road end of the pasture. The two hunters were sprawled out flat, taking every advantage of their summer's rest. The yearlings were behind old Knock, he heard them stamping.

He shook his head. He must get up. He positioned his front legs, heaved his hind quarters under him. One more effort and he was standing. As he sauntered over to the water trough set between this field and the one that contained the brood mares and new foals, his off-hind leg dragged stiffly. He ignored the discomfort, knowing the stiffness would ease with exercise.

The yearlings suddenly acquired thirst too and frolicked about him as he made his stately way, ignoring their antics. The brown came a bit too near him and the old grey horse extended his neck, teeth bared, to put the brown in mind of his manners.

Knock blew across the surface of the trough, rippling away dust and leaves. He touched the water, cool on his lips, and then plunged his nose in to suck deeply. The first water of the day was the best and he took his fill.

The younger stock, donkeys included, crowded in to the water. The old horse backed carefully away and began to search, head down, to sniff out any sweet blades he might have missed in yesterday's grazing.

He had filled his stomach for the first time that day before he heard any activity in the farmyard. As was his habit these past seasons, he wandered towards the house, breasting the fence that separated the fields from the gardens and orchard about the neat bungalow. The fence, so neatly painted that spring, showed grimy patches where he leaned into it, opposite the window where she often appeared. The window was blank, curtains drawn.

He gazed towards the barnyard now, to the figures carrying the morning feeds to the whickering horses in the stable row. He neighed softly, hopefully, but no one turned to wave at him. He looked back at the window: sometimes, after he called, he could see movement: a hand or a white face as the edge of the curtain was pulled aside. Sometimes, the blankness lifted completely and he could see the outline of her familiar figure. He hadn't seen her in some time: not since the hard weather eased into a wet spring. He snorted with disappointment and stamped the ground. He stamped again, tossing his head, and noticed long grass stems just on the other side of the fence. By a careful angling of his long head, he could just reach the grass. He contented himself with nibbling all along the fence by the houseyard. She might just still come out to him with a carrot, or an apple, or even a slice of bread if he stayed by the fence long enough.

The flurry of activity in the horse yard ended as the three men went back into the house, leaving the stabled horses munching.

Philosophically old Knock finished cropping the other side of the fence and then moved off. If she didn't visit him in the morning, she often came out with the others in the evening when all the stock was checked.

He was half asleep in the sun when shouts and a scrabble of shod hooves on stone brought his head up and ears pricking towards the stable yard. A big bay mare was dancing about, eluding the rider who wished to mount her. The old horse wondered why she bothered: she only delayed the inevitable. He heaved a sigh.

It had been a long time since he'd felt a rider's weight. She hadn't ridden him, even gently about the fields, since last summer. No one else had ridden him since that day. He looked again at her window and it was still blank.

The mare was still trying to have her way, rearing and prancing, the men shouting in the hard determined way he remembered. He heard the splat of crop on flesh; the mare hesitated and her rider vaulted across the saddle. Another splat brought an abrupt end to the contest. She had never had to use a stick on him, he remembered complacently. Always he had been ready to do as she asked, for she'd a light hand, a firm seat and a kind voice. They'd gone like the wind together across field and through forest. Those had been the good days: when he'd breath and will to run, when his muscles moved easily, when he couldn't wait to see what the next field brought, ditch or fence or bank, the baying of the hounds ahead of them and most of the other, slower horses stretched out behind them. She'd been a light and gracious burden for him to carry, her hands along his neck encouraging him, her affectionate pulling at his ears (which he had permitted only her to do), the slaps of approval on his neck when the day had ended. And the tidbits from her hand as she saw him safely bedded for the night inside a warm, deep-strawed stable.

He'd had other riders from time to time: some he'd carried with no protest. There had been the odd one or two he hadn't wanted on his back. He developed a simple trick of dropping his shoulder or going under a low limb at speed. Those times were few because, mostly, she rode him. He could take pride in the knowledge that he had never failed her, nor faltered no matter what she had asked him to jump or do.

The bay's rider had now guided the mare into the practice ring where the old grey horse had so often been worked with her on his back. The rider put the mare into the old remembered drill of walk, trot, canter, cross the arena, walk, trop, stop, back, jog, canter which was so familiar to the old horse that the skin across his ribs twitched. He could almost feel the pressure of the saddle on his withers, the girth firm under his belly. He watched, head up and ears pricked, as the schooling continued. Then the rider turned the mare towards the jumps set up in the training field.

As he watched the mare, the old horse could almost hear her voice in his ears, encouraging him, praising him as they careered about the field and over the obstacles. She'd steady him with her voice when the excitement of performance overcame his normal calm. She'd laugh when he'd buck out over the last fence, as if she knew how glad he was to have gone clear. He remembered, and the skin of his chest rippled, how he'd be jarred to his poll sometimes by the hardness of the ground as he landed after a big fence. Best of all, he had liked the spreads, for then he had seemed to be suspended briefly between ground and sky. That sensation he had liked above all, spurning the earth in those scant seconds as if he might one day leap with her to the sun itself had he the right ground for take-off.

Best yet were the times he'd stood with other horses and permitted ribbons to be attached to his browband. He could sense, even through the leather of the saddle, her pride and joy.

The bruff-bruff high blowing of the mare brought him back from his dreaming. She'd been checked for the second spread: he heard the rattling tattoo of her hooves as she pulled to be free, the silence of her take-off and the grunt of landing as she cantered on.

"Ross!" He heard someone shouting from the front of the house. He pricked his ears forward, straining as the call was repeated: it sounded like her voice, but it wasn't. He stamped, disappointed. She used to watch them jump other horses. He knew she was in the house, behind that blank window. Why didn't she come and see him?

The mare and her rider had turned, cantering back to the gate into the stable yard where the other woman waited. The man jumped from the mare's back.

"Ross, she wouldn't even take her tea this morning. I've called the doctor. He's coming right over."

The urgency, the ripple of fear in the woman's voice, so like the voice he longed to hear, made the old horse whicker hopefully. He whuffled again when he saw them turn their heads in his direction. "Oh, Ross, how could old Knock know?"

"Don't be silly, Mairéad. He couldn't know. He's always at the fence in the morning. Mam used to feed him when she was still able. It's just habit, that's all, Mairéad."

"It isn't as if we weren't expecting it, Ross, but somehow . . ."

"Just let me put the mare up."

Knock watched as the two parted, the man leading the bay mare back to her stable. As the woman slowly walked towards him, he nickered softly.

"Do you know, Knock? Mam always said you were smart for a horse." She extended her hand to his questing lips. "D'you know Mam's dying?"

Her hand was empty but she stroked his nose. He sensed her unhappiness and stood quietly as she leaned her forehead against his neck. She'd done that sometimes, standing with her head against him, hands quiescent on his nose and shoulder; sometimes, too, as this woman did now, she'd made funny noises and left his shoulder wet.

"Oh, Knock, when I think of how she used to be . . . and then to see her now, in pain, so weak . . ."

Knock heard the man's footsteps but he didn't move.

"If Knock were in such pain, we could put him down so he needn't suffer . . ."

"Ross, how could you say such a thing . . ."

"It'd be kinder, wouldn't it?" The man's voice sounded angry. "Wouldn't it, Mairéad? D'you think I don't realise what Mam's going through? It's a rotten dirty trick to pull on a gallant old lady, but at least she can die in her own bed, with her own friends about and . . ."

"Knock waiting for her at the fence."

The woman whirled from Knock, crying with emotion that the old horse smelled so acutely he blew softly in reaction. The man had his arms about the woman, comforting her with small pats on her shoulders and soft words. As he stood that way, his eyes caught the old horse's, almost accusingly.

The horse heard the car first, lifting his head, seeing the bright flash of its blue paint through the trees that bordered the drive. The woman broke from the comforting arms and ran across the grass towards the front of the house to intercept the car.

"It would be kinder," the man said in a low voice, staring at the horse, "but we can't, can we? You'll miss her, too, won't you, lad?" He slapped Knock affectionately on the neck before he walked quickly after the woman.

The first car heralded the arrival of many: some discharging passengers and leaving, while others parked on the front lawn and tarmacadam. Pleased by the unusual activity to entertain him, the old horse wondered what was to happen. So many cars generally meant a sale of animals or a show in the big jumping field. Today, however, no teams of people bustled about setting up jumps and roping off arenas for rings. The uneasy aura about the house made him restless and he couldn't settle to grazing with yearlings. Almost as if he hoped to find some subtle comfort, he drifted to his usual spot at the fence. Her window was occluded but now and then the curtains moved as someone brushed by them.

Obscurely troubled, the old horse stamped his off-fore. As if his action were some sort of cue, he heard the faint sound of distressed cries, of loud weeping. The curtains now bounced with agitation and he thought for a brief moment that they would at last be pulled aside and he'd see her. The movement ceased but the noises, muffled though they were by the walls of the house, carried clearly to his ears. He didn't like the sounds and he stamped again in his nervousness. He wanted to leave the fence side but some unheard restraint compelled him to remain in vigil. Abruptly the compulsion ceased. Free to move, he did not. He waited by the fence.

Full of grass and bored of sportive play, the yearlings came over for a while midafternoon. They made a great show of fear and galloped off when a car came round the house to park on the tarmacadam in the rere. Knock maintained his dignified stance.

"Mick, surely that's not Maeve's old Knock still alive?"

The sound of the woman's voice, slightly familiar to him, made the old horse turn his head, ears moving. He whuffled softly as she came up to him. She had dug a sugar lump from one pocket and held out her hand flatly so politely he extended his neck to accept her offering.

"You never supposed Maeve would sell that fella to the factory, did you?" asked the man with a lightly derisive laugh. He ran a practised hand from Knock's shoulder to his neck and gave him an admiring slap. "Not with all those winnings she collected on him!"

"But Mick, he's surely over thirty?"

"Suspect he is. In grand shape for all of that." The man's tone changed abruptly. "C'mon. We'd better go in. Get it over with."

"A minute, Mick. I've found another bit of sugar." She fumbled in her pocket and held the battered offering under Knock's nose. He gave a sniff but lipped it up willingly. She patted his cheek. "Poor old fella. No one's had time for you today, I'll bet." Her voice quavered and Knock tensed, catching the note of emotion.

"Now, Sally . . ."

"I know, Mick," and the woman gave a convulsive sob now, "it was just seeing old Knock waiting by her window and no way to tell him . . ."

No sooner had the two hurried around to the front of the

house than another car arrived in the rere. Knock regarded the new arrivals with keen interest as they emerged from the car. There might be more sugar lumps.

"B'Gawd, he's there. Tol'ya he'd be," said a thickened voice which Knock allied with the man who used to shoe his feet. "You and your notions that the one would die with the other?" He scoffed loudly and was ordered to hush by his companions. He glanced at the curtained window and hunched his shoulders up to his neck, feigning repentance. "B'Gawd, though, he'd fetch a fine price at Straffan, now wouldn't he, Joe?"

The men were close enough to him now for Knock to smell the sourness he distrusted. He had always associated that odour with trouble and a groom he'd hated. He blew out in distress and backed away from the fence.

"Jesus, if the old horse didn't understand ya, Joe!" The other two men pulled the farrier along with them to the front of the house. "Mind your mush inside t'house, for Gaw'd sake!"

Warily observing their progress away from him, Knock noticed that the windows of the big room overlooking the field were not blank. He could see the white faces turned in his direction and, ears waggling at the muted sounds of voices, he watched the watchers until the next car came around. He stepped back to his position at the fence, head up, ears forward. But the people were too occupied with conveying bowls, trays and crates, though he caught the unmistakable odour of the food they carried briskly through the kitchen door.

The skies were darkening now and a chill wind blew raggedly up from the sea, an unusual direction at this time of the year. The young horses joined Knock, pressing against his bulk for some warmth. The hunters, aloof, chose a place along the fence nearer the stables.

Suddenly half a dozen people came out the back door, hoarsely reassuring the woman who remained in the opening. Then she saw Knock and, with a startled cry, slammed the door shut.

There was a lot of bustle and calling and banging in the stable yard as the volunteers coped with feeding unfamiliar horses and the arrangements of a strange barn.

"Hey, get a scoop for old Knock, too. He deserves a feed at this wake if anyone does!"

A man approached the old horse, a scoop held at waist level. The smell of nuts reassured Knock more than this stranger's soothing words. The scoop was only half full but Knock was grateful. The yearlings, naturally, came to see what was happening. Laughing softly, the man gave them the odd few so that they wouldn't steal from Knock.

Sunset was obcured by a mizzling rain, following the rise of bluster in that seaborne wind. Knock maintained his hopeful position at the fence but no more cars came round to the rere though there was enough coming and going down the drive to the main road. When the dampness soaked through to chill his back, Knock sought shelter with the others against the hedgerow where the trees lining the driveway gave some protection. The yearlings pressed around him for comfort and warmth.

Not only did the weather deteriorate but the headlights and noise of cars constantly up and down the drive kept rousing the horses from the little rest they could get.

Towards morning, the wind dropped and the rain eased off. The yearlings moved away, grazing to comfort their cold bellies, but Knock was too stiff to move. He longed for the sun to warm and ease his cold back and stiff hind leg. There had been a time when she would have him brought in under cover on such a night as this.

Knock was resentful as well as miserable and, acting from habit, he stiffly moved towards her window and, lifting his head, whinnied sharply. Abruptly the curtain was pulled back from the window. He blinked against the sudden sharp brightness. He whinnied again. The curtain was abruptly dropped into place, though a thin edge of light showed at one side. Then the kitchen door opened and three figures came out.

"Knock? Is that you, fella? How did you know, fella? How did you know?"

Knock recognised the voice of the bay's rider and whickered again as the three men approached him. Then the wind brought to his nostrils the sour smell he hated and, despite the kindness and the sorrow in the blurred voice, he backed away.

"He was cold, that's all it is, Ross," said the thick voice of the farrier. He bent to climb through the slats of the fence. "I'll just catch him up and put him in the barn."

Knock threw up his head, whinnying both fear and warning. He wanted no part of someone smelling like that. He wheeled sharply on his hindquarters, though his stiff leg nearly buckled, as he ran from the smell and the men. When he felt safely out of their reach, he turned to see if they intended to follow him. They were silhouetted now for someone had thrown back the curtains of her window. He called once more. The curtain fell back and then even the edge of light went out.

He tossed his head, blowing. She had not heard him. She did not even come to the window. He was very unhappy. Disconsolately he plodded off to join the yearlings. They were better than no company on this disturbing cold night when she no longer heard him.

RICHARD LLEWELLYN

Irish Joys

I heaved my suitcase through the window and, turning to tip the porter, I saw along the train Niamh O'Sharranna's knees — a beautiful sight — jostling her skirts in a run for the Guard's van, because we were gently on the move, and the Guard held out a hand to pull her aboard, and the two porters threw her bags in, and the train went round the curve. I was so happy to know I had someone to talk to and even drink with on the two-and-a-half day journey to Bariloche.

I had often wondered about her surname. Her O'Sharranna ancestor had been an officer of an Irish regiment, part of a British force invading Argentina back in the 18-somethings, that went down narrow streets under fire of Gaucho troops on the rooftops of the capital, and with full-headed tenacity marched into certain destruction, but at some time, the Irish troops — without any love for the English — went off into the side streets and, not very far away, were out in the Pampas. They made friends easily, for they were all skilled farmhands, masons and builders, and there was plenty of work, and they flourished.

O'Sharranna had joined the Argentinian Army for the Desert War against the Indios, and under General Wynter he served throughout, and got a one-hundred-mile square of Pampas land as a gift for his services. He bought tracts on both sides, and north and south, from his comrades, and after a few years he had a demesne that would take five days of hard riding to cross diagonally. He passed on to his son a flock of thirty thousand sheep, and eight thousand cattle — recorded in his diaries — and died a millionaire in gold pesos.

The family married here and there, but man or woman they never changed the surname. Yet how O'Sharranna came to be was lost in the records, and since clerks of that day were not averse to using their quills as they wished, then O'Sharranna could have been anything, depending on an illiterate cowpat ear. Still, the name carried weight. Niamh must have been wealthy in her own right, but she had preferred to study nursing in London, and returned to Buenos Aires to become assistant matron at a famous hospital.

She had no notion how her name came to be and was not in the slightest degree interested. It was a name revered in most parts and that was enough, as she had told me. We met at the house of friends — Cathal and Brid Taylor — years before, but I left the country for Australia to manage a sheep farm, and when it ended I refused a longer term and went back to the Pampas, my silent love. It is said that if you eat the berry, you will have to return. It is true. I know it. That was why I was on the train. I had no prospect of a job, but I knew I was wanted somewhere. I knew sheep and wool better than most, and cattle better than some. I knew I was wanted. That was enough.

I had paperwork, a thesis on sheep and cattle, and books. I had plenty to do and to read. But there is a fascination about looking out of a window and seeing familiar places pass by and thinking of the people you know living there, and hearing the engine's whistle carry you past, and being sorry you must go on without a rap on the door and a greeting. But there, a greeting means two or three weeks before you may go, and every day a wonderful holiday with all the neighbours coming in to put their arms about you as a friend, and feasts of grilled lamb on iron stakes, and wine from the cask, and any trick to keep you from going, because you are from the outside world and they love your every word, savouring it as a joyous message.

As I thought, she came in on the first call for dinner and hurried to me with outflung arms. I looked into those bluest-of-blue eyes, and all the yearnings and churnings of the years gone by came back and I could barely let her go. When she sat down she had a rosier colour, so I knew she felt the same emotion, and it was a lovely feeling, and I ordered a bottle of champagne with the *asado* of baby beef, and two martinis to begin.

I let her do the talking and there was such a lot to say, and when it was my turn, I told her about Melbourne and Sydney, and the Outback, and the aborigines, and throwing boomerangs, and the rest of it.

"But what an interesting life!" she said, and opened her hands. "What have *I* done? Walked the wards. Night duty. Operations. Fevers. Injections. Now I'm taking a month off to stay with my sister on the shores of Lake Nahuel Huapi, near the mouth of the Leman, and I'm going to fish. D'you like fishing?"

"Love it!"

"Come and stay with us. I promise you salmon, rainbow trout, perch, anything you like. And you won't find an hotel to touch it for food or anything else. On?"

"Expect me. How're things with Cathal and Brid?"

The bluest-of-blue looked at me direct, a matron's stare. "How long have you been out of the country?" she asked, and turned to the window, and her eyes twitched with the passing scenery. "You've heard nothing about them?"

"Nothing. Why?"

"Not important enough, obviously." She sat back, playing with a spoon. "Remember they had a little Indio girl there? As a companion for their own daughter?"

"A little dark thing, yes."

"Cathal was going to adopt her, but Brid hated the idea from the start. She didn't want to. She flew to Buenos Aires to see the family lawyer. He was so horrified, he took the plane back with her and tried with all his might to change Cathal's mind. But he was the stubborn Irish variety, and never mind that Brid wept and screamed, he insisted. The lawyer told him what would happen legally. An adopted child is protected by Argentinian law, and it's very strict. It automatically becomes a co-inheritor. It, in this case, the little Indio. I've told you I never had the slightest liking for her. I love children, but not that one. She was sly as the Patagonian fox. The governess they engaged for Grainne was German, with absolute tutorial command of the syllabus. She was a thoroughly good woman, and she got excellent results from the daughter. But when I stayed there for a few days, I had a talk with Frau von Beck, and she told me that the Indio was a stone — she pounded the table with her fist — and that she was holding Grainne back."

The waiter served a remarkable steak, perfectly grilled over charcoal, and poured the fine wine from Mendoza I'd chosen instead of the champagne. We know about most European wines but we never hear of those from Argentina. The best are equal to any of the others because the vines come from the best of Europe's vineyards, and sun, soil and nature do the rest.

"Well, Cathal had his way," Niamh said. "The governess was dismissed. There was a tremendous party to see the little thing sign her name in the book — big letters and I can see them now — poking her tongue out to make the shapes, and the scream that went up from the Indios, two or three thousand of them from everywhere, would ruin your ears. Why not? They had a princess. Why not? They only had to wait. By using that pen, she owned half of everything. In Argentina *and* Europe, remember."

The waiter served a soufflé of sliced peaches, certainly not the simplest thing to cook on a train, but we were then still in the waning heyday of the British tradition, and it died hard, thank God.

"Brid came to accept it almost apathetically, because — as she told me — a half, properly administered, would give Grainne far more than she would need to live in comfort, and she certainly was not brought up to dip a snout in the fleshpots. Anyway, she went off to school in Switzerland, and the little thing was sent to a convent school up in Tucuman. The nuns' reports did nothing to raise Cathal's spirits. They were incapable of dealing with her, either in the classroom or in the house and playground. She was a troublemaker, and she clawed. Other parents were beginning to complain. Cathal collected all the nuns' reports and took them to his lawyer to annul the adoption. But Argentine law isn't simple. With the Indios' lawyers fighting it, it could take a long time. Perhaps years, if then. Indios had a deep root in the country, and the courts had the job of protecting them as a sacred duty. By that time, after the talks with his lawyers, Cathal was a sick and sorry one. He and Brid went over to Europe to see Grainne, and the business went on of trying to shift that little thing out of her place."

I told her that I had some experience of the law and its way of dragging things out. We had been run down in Sydney Harbour by a bigger ship, but it took two years and a nudge from a Minister to sort things out and get our money.

"Nothing but a closed brotherhood anywhere," Niamh said. "A blackguardly lot. They rear up when you say it, but it's true enough. It *is.* Well, Cathal and Brid came back for the shearing. It's an important time, as you know. When the wool prices are fixed, they know what's coming in for the year."

The waiter served coffee and I ordered two cognacs, and we tried to make what we called Irish Joys by mixing them, and I must say they were such a success that I ordered two more.

"Yes, now, where was I?" Niamh said, in a curious stare at the goblet. "Well, it was always Brid's way to go into the local town on a Friday to buy stores for the house and the shepherds and bring it all back in the van. That night she got back at about nine. Dinner was ready as usual but Cathal wasn't there, and the maid seemed to think he'd gone up to Number Two shearing shed, about twenty miles away. Brid waited for an hour. Then she went across to the house of the Capataz, the chief herdsman, and got him out of bed. Sleep early, up early. But he knew nothing about Cathal, and he certainly hadn't been at the shearing shed since seven o'clock. It was then eleven. Brid thought of a breakdown or a burst tyre, and she told the Capataz to bring a couple of his men for a fast ride to the sheds, expecting to meet Cathal on the way. They didn't find him. The sheds were dark. Nobody had seen him. They didn't see him on the way back. He wasn't at the house. Brid was frantic. She telephoned the commander of the Garrison and he promised to bring out a squad of Gendarmeria at first light, and to warn the helicopter squadron."

She drank her second Irish Joy in sips. Waiters were clearing away, but people stayed on to smoke and talk, and the train picked up speed.

"As you may have guessed, he was never found," she said. "A reward of a million pesos was offered in the papers and on the radio. But? Nothing. I was brought into it because the lawyer staying down there called me, and said Brid was quite out of her mind, and would I take charge, and so I did. She was in the clinic with me for a couple of months. In all that time, not a word. I knew the wink was going round that he'd met somebody and taken her to Europe, and he'd be back. But it's difficult to leave Argentina without papers, permits, currency certificates and the rest of it. There was no record anywhere, sea, land or air. A mystery. The lawyer, a thoroughly good man, commanded her to go back to Europe and to stay there a minimum of two years, and he put a Patagonian Welshman, a first-class manager, in charge of the farm. He more than proved himself the first year. First, he got rid of the men he didn't want. Too long they had been winesotted and indolent. Nobody looking after things, you see? Then he threw out the little thing's father, a bone-lazy brute who thought he could do as he pleased because his daughter was personally half-owner. There was the devil of a row about it, but the Gendarmeria were always about the place, and if they put you in the lock-up, be sure it will be months before you are out. But in the meantime, Gwil Lewis had got from every part of Patagonia the finest team of trackers in the land. Some were Tehuelche and others Mapuche, and a couple from the south, Onan. They could tell you the height, weight and colour of the horse, and the height of the man and what he was wearing. They could tell you the make and model of the van, and if the driver had on gloves. I'm not saying how, but that's the sort of tracker. *Amazing!*"

I ordered a couple more, and slid a note under the tray to make sure we were not disturbed.

"Do you want to hear the rest of this?" she asked.

"Of course. After all, I knew them!"

She gave me full benefit of a bluest-of-blue matronal stare. I think I know how nurses feel.

"I told you about the trackers. Some of them brought their sons with them. Smart as their fathers. After the shearing, Gwil took a team of fence-menders and started at the southwest post. He rode two days ahead with his trackers, first, to keep their tracks out of any he might find, and second, to have time to repair posts and wire. As he told me, he was reasoning that Cathal had never left the farm. Killed and hidden, is what he said. He brought the trackers out to prove it. Well, they were out about five weeks, always near the fence, and close in. But nothing to show. They found nothing. Nobody expected them to. It was more than a year, and the wind will cover any track. Except from the eyes of the tracker. One of the sons saw the track first, took of his boots — bare feet can be told apart from any other track — and his father joined him, and they rested hands on a bent knee, and they looked. Gwil told me he sat there and puffed his pipe. They read that track as we read a book and they looked away and pointed. They all followed steady till night, and they lit a fire to grill a lamb, and bake bread, and have a drink of wine. Trackers never say what they have seen until they have found what they are looking for, so there was no talk, and they turned in, and up before first light, and by sunrise they were going southeast by Gwil's compass, at least a hundred and seventy miles from the House. Gwil thought there was no need to stay with them now they were on the track, so he left with a couple of the horse handlers and he was home four days later. He was surprised to be told that Brid and her lawyers and accountants had arrived some days before with a troop of Gendarmeria, and they were all at the house with the wool and hides people. Well, Gwil had a say there because he was on a percentage of everything, so he went down for a drink and took his figures, and met Brid, and they had a good talk. He told her nothing of finding a track. It was raising a hope, and if it was only that, it was obvious she could never sustain it. She was thin, and lacksadaisy, nothing like the girl she had been. The grief, he said, stuck from every bone."

The steward or waiter, whatever they are called, looked at me brows up, and I nodded for two more.

"You knew Brid," Niamh said. "She was always one for the free air and a gallop to test the horse, and back for breakfast. The officer commanding the Gendarmeria had expressly forbidden her to ride without escort. The morning after Gwil got back, she was out before dawn, so the gauchos said. She never came back."

Tears pushed through her eyelashes and she wiped them away with a lace-fringed handkerchief, a lovely bit of *femme* I was simply not used to.

"Everything seemed to go to the devil," she said, quietly. "Snows had gathered in the Andes, they swelled the River Chubut that flowed through the estate. Tracking was hopeless in the rise of the water, so the tracking team went home. And no sign of Brid. Days of disaster and hysteria. But made much worse by the arrival of Grainne. She flew in on Aerolineas with the Irish Consul-General and an escort. What could be done? Take the sheep and cattle to the high ground, but what else? Well, the Garrison Commander was very interested in the fact that nobody had informed to win the reward of a million pesos. This is no small sum. It made him think it was an inside job by the Indios. If the little thing became, in fact, the part-heiress, they could sell the estate for many millions more and share it between them. You know, there is nothing so steady as the Indio. He doesn't want to understand, he never will. Your laws are not his. With his eyes he tells you to go to hell. He thinks he knows what is right. Every rock, every leaf, every bit of grass tells him so. They *talk* to each other. That is their strength. Gringo money? To them, nothing. But to sell land they regard as their own, pilfered from them, with the sheep and cattle they have cared for, ah, yes. It was theirs through their princess. It was legal. All the lawyers said so. Therefore? All they had to do was wait. They had always waited, and they were used to it."

The steward put down the two drinks and went back to turn out, pointedly, I thought, all the other lamps except the two over our table.

Lights from a passing train flitted her face with strange shadows that went as she lifted the glass.

"Well, you must have guessed what happened next," she said, putting the glass down slowly, carefully. "Did you?"

"Grainne disappeared?"

"Exactly. How, nobody knew. Soldiers, Gendarmeria, all the farmers and their gauchos, they made a long line to search for tracks. Nothing. They covered every inch, fence to fence. The river had gone down, the land was dry, everything was in their favour. But? Nothing. Then something strange happened, on the very day the Governor and his staff were there having lunch. You remember the Onan tracker? He arrived there, and he told the Governor that now the river was down, he could go back to where he hammered in a stick and follow the track. Nobody believed him, of course. The river over its banks for more than three months, and he could follow track? It took four days to ride there, and they set up a camp. They could all see the stick, because a river rises, it doesn't send waves. Onan are water men, the sea and the river are one to them. That man went to the stick and started going a pace at a time. The rest kept back. He was going into the marsh. It can go deep. Only the horsemen could see him over the bulrushes and reeds. I was there in case Grainne was found. The lawyer sent for me, and I'm glad I went. Indios make sad mistakes.

When she went, the river was going down. The marsh was still treacherous. Obviously she was lassoed and tied to her horse, a big stallion, and he was driven in, but not far enough. He kicked his way to a drier part where he could feed. That man, the Onan, found them first, and then he found Cathal and Brid. They were in a deep sump, dug out almost a hundred years before to bury the rubbish of the house. Grainne was in a dreadful state of course, but after three weeks in the intensive care unit, she was able to fly to Paris. I'm just back from taking her to the care of her aunt there."

"And the little black thing?"

"Poor little soul. The last school she was at simply sent her back. She gave herself all the airs of a princess, because that's how her own people treated her. Gringo education, or any attempt to accustom her to what we'd call proper behaviour was not her way. So they sent her back. Her parents had a shanty on the outskirts of the estate. But she wanted to live as the nuns had taught her. Cleanliness, laundry. You see, some lessons go deep down. The arrest of the family and the gauchos on the farm was ordered by the Governor, and he packed them all off to the province of the Onan. That's in the far south. Somebody cut her throat, and she was found burned in the ashes of the shanty."

She stood, and drank the last drops.

"You see, it's simply the old story all over again," she said, but so sadly. "Irishmen can make the large gesture, and provide the world with an example of Christian kindness and all that. Cathal was thinking of public acclaim, the priest's blessing and the rest. He wasn't thinking of his own family. They were last in his mind. A hopeless romantic, like so many of us. Aren't we a funny lot? Thank you for a lovely dinner. Good night, and *sláinte*. See you at Nahuel Huapi!"

PETER LUKE

Point Of No Return

For June Tobin

Castlemore in south County Wexford is described in the tourist brochures as a 'pleasant seaside resort with a fine view of the celebrated Saltee Islands'. Possibly it has never achieved the renown of other such places of amenity because of its sad associations with the Wexford Rising. For Castlemore's only two geographical features are respectively named Transportation Quay and Point of No Return.

Nevertheless, out of the whole wide world these two handsome widowed sisters had chosen Castlemore for their summer holiday. It was, in the first place, a matter of family history; their forebear, Dinny Joe Rossiter, had lived there before being transported to Van Dieman's Land for his participation in the aforementioned Rebellion of '98. The result was the subsequent founding of the Australian Rossiter clan. More than one hundred and seventy years later two of the family, Hilda and Maeve, happened to meet an Irish priest in Sydney who had been born in County Wexford. He was a certain Father Cullen who mentioned in the course of conversation that he had a sister living in Castlemore who let rooms to summer visitors. That is how it started.

The Rossiter sisters were, or had been, two big bouncing Aussie girls born in a large family in New South Wales. Forty years or so had taken some of the bounce but none of the edge out of Hilda. Maeve was considerably younger and, until recently, had happily assumed that God (a Catholic) put in a twenty-four-hour day in His Heaven seeing to it that all was well with the world.

Hilda was a war widow who had known her airforce husband only a few months when, bound, blindfolded and on his knees, he had had his head struck from his young neck by a Japanese officer's sword. Malaya, 1942, that was. Maeve, the youngest of the family, had made her marriage in the post-war years and translated to London with her husband when work took him there. It was in London that her two boys, now aged eleven and seven, had been born, and it was in London that their father, in his full puissance as husband and bread-winner, had, with a surprised and slightly angry expression on his face, died quite suddenly of a fairly rare disease.

Hearing the news, Hilda had at once flown to London to comfort Maeve in her distress. Maeve's distress was great but, being a woman of spirit who still had her health and more than her share of looks, she decided from the first to make the best of the situation.

The Rossiters were Aussies since the days of Botany Bay but, like other such families, they had kept something of their Irishness by importing the occasional relative from the Old Country as well as by marrying within the Celtic community of the new one.

"I'll tell you what we'll do," Maeve said to Hilda as soon as the obsequies were over, "we'll go for a couple of weeks to Ireland."

"Why Ireland?" said Hilda, who had not become reconciled to the climate. "What's the matter with New South Wales?"

"Ah, come on, Hilda," said the younger sister, "we could go to Wexford where the family originally came from. We might even find some relations there."

"Who wants relations," replied the elder, "when we've got an epidemic of them in New South Wales?"

"But think how nice it would be for the kids to be able to say they had been to Ireland. It would be good for them to have a bit of sea air after London."

"Don't expect it to be like Bondi Beach, that's all," said Hilda by way of conceding the point.

And so the two widows, together with Maeve's small sons, Eamonn and Anthony, caught the packet to Rosslare and in due course arrived at Father Cullen's sister's damp house near Castlemore. There they stared out through salt encrusted window-panes at the rain which blanketed out the view of the Saltees and everything else besides. Nor did they feel much comfort in Miss Cullen's announcement that each bed in the house had been blessed by a priest of God.

During these early house-bound hours Maeve amused herself by speculating about the Australian ethos. Did the generic Aussie character, she wondered, derive from an Irish word, flahoolick, which, as someone had once told her, meant princely? Or did it come about from over-exposure to down-under sun? Of course, all people (like the Irish) born and bred in exile (like the Rossiters) create their own myth of what they wished they were, or how they think they ought to be.

We, the Rossiters — so she reasoned — have always regarded ourselves as a friendly, jolly, come-day-go-day sort of crowd "because we are Irish". But here in Ireland just how Irish are we?

When Hilda and Maeve, the first Rossiters for nearly two centuries to return to Ireland, did make landfall at Castlemore they were in fact rather surprised at the reception they got — or, more precisely, the reception that they did not get. It is possible that Maeve in her naïve Aussie heart had something like a wolfhound and a band of girl pipers in mind. As a direct descendant of a Rossiter who had been up in '98 with Father Murphy of Boulavogue, why not? Indeed as flesh and blood of the bould Dinny Joe who had fought with the Shelmaliers and Bargymen at Vinegar Hill was she not entitled to a few romantic notions?

Hilda, on the other hand, cynical from long and sterile conjunction with the Australian male, vaguely imagined a crowd of Victor McLaglens playing pitch-and-toss at the cross-roads and — at least on Fair days — hitting each other over the head with blackthorn sticks while the wives, of course, starved in ditches. Well, perhaps not quite . . . but neither of them, certainly, expected things to be the way they actually were.

They were received with the utmost courtesy, of course; but no smiles, no pumping handshakes — not even the eyebrow of recognition at the mention of the local name of Rossiter. Indeed, the only sort of hearty welcome they received was from a streel of tinker children temporarily occupying the nearby sand dunes. These, as soon as motherly Maeve had admired their tow coloured heads, gave her typically the 'panny-for-the-babby' treatment and she, equally typically, coughed up over-generously. The travelling children then laid siege to the house until Miss Cullen threatened them with the Civic Guard. Thereafter they lay in wait among the junked cars in the field behind the house. This was at first alarming for Eamonn and Anthony reared in Swiss Cottage; then for their suburban Sydney auntie when the boys developed a taste for tinker life. Botany Bay bate the lot, she thought.

As for the rest of the Castlemore community, they were

adroit at scrutinising without seeming to stare. The women were avid with curiosity about the visitors, yet when Maeve turned to give them a friendly smile their heads and eyes were elsewhere. As for the men, they did not seem to be aware of the newcomers. Certainly they did not appear to acknowledge, however discreetly, the fact that there were now two fine-looking women in their midst where before there had been none. As Hilda said, they would probably have made a more concupiscent inspection of a pair of Raleigh bicycles.

Maeve, a compulsive shopper, was the sort of person who could not have landed on the moon without finding the need to pop in to buy something — if only some washing-up liquid or a bottle of moisturiser. Now the kids' gobs needed stopping with Crunchies and their developing minds with comics. In the village shop the appearance of Hilda and Maeve was electrifying (one cannot see electricity — only feel it) and the buzz of conversation did not stop: it was more like a radio being turned low. All the same, Maeve's cheerful greeting was not only acknowledged with punctilio by Miss Harvey, the proprietor, it was taken up in muttered chorus by other lady-shoppers as well. The children, with their quick perceptions however, sensed that Mummy's friendly, indeed beautiful smile, was somehow too much — like a woman in full evening dress where everyone else was in denims.

"Ireland of the Welcomes I don't think!" said Hilda when they were outside and on their way to the strand.

"What's that?" asked the other.

"Irish Tourist Board hand-out to do with the contraction of face muscles. It's called smiling."

"But everyone's very polite," Maeve protested, determined to be pleased with the place.

"I'd feel more at home if they bit me," answered the elder sister.

Like everything else they had so far seen in Ireland, the strand, when they got there, was a surprise. In the first place it was long and clean and sandy. Secondly, it was quite deserted, or seemingly so.

"Oh, it's lovely!" exclaimed Maeve, comparing it with recent memories of the English south coast.

"Yes," said Hilda, "just like Bondi — all those beautiful sunburned bodies! I suppose that hunk of beefcake there is the Life Guard?" Hilda pointed down the beach to where a gaunt old man in a black cap was staring out to sea. "At first I thought it was a piece of driftwood stood on end."

In fact, as they now saw, the place was not deserted. Above the high-waterline, seated on rocks and on the soft sand of the dunes, were several people, both men and women, in dark clothing, who moved little and spoke not at all. But, of bathers and holiday-makers there was no sign.

"Who are those people?" asked Eamonn.

"I don't know, darling. Locals, I suppose. Fishermen, probably."

"But are the women fishermen?" persisted Anthony.

"I don't suppose so, darling. They're probably just people who live by the sea."

"They never seem to talk," said Eamonn. "You told me the Irish talk all the time."

"Mummy, don't they have tourists in Ireland?" asked the younger child.

"Yes, of course, darling."

"Where are they, then?"

"Benidorm or Torremolinos if they've got any sense," cracked Hilda.

"The attraction of Ireland for tourists is miles and miles of empty beaches like this one," said Maeve.

"Very clever! And this, I suppose, is what they call the Height of the Season?" said Hilda. "If you ask me that old ancestor of ours was on to a good thing — free ticket to Tasmania and all found."

"Oh, come off it, Hilda," said Maeve. "It's different — look?" And she pointed to where her two boys, already tiny specks tearing across the wet sand, were chasing a flock of sanderlings which, unwilling to be put to flight, kept running before them like clockwork toys. Beyond was the horizon, a pale vanishing-point between sea and sky where, as they watched, the rain belt drew to one side like a gauze curtain, revealing the Saltee Islands, first one and then the other, washed clean and hung out to dry in the sun.

"I don't care what you say, Hilda," insisted Maeve, "that's

really beautiful."

Back at Miss Cullen's the beds were damp and smelt of urine.

"Take a sniff of that," said Hilda to her sister.

"What is it?" asked Maeve dubiously.

"You're a mother, you should know," answered the other.

"So that's what Miss Cullen meant by being blessed by a priest of God," said Maeve, suddenly helpless with laughter — laughter in which the boys joined, covering their mouths with their hands, until long after the joke was over.

"You know," said Maeve to her sister later that evening, "I used to think of myself as a special sort of Irishwoman. It's taken this trip for me to realise that I'm one hundred per cent Australian after all."

The next day was fine and Maeve and the boys decided to go for a swim.

The tide was coming in when they got to the strand and the regiments of small white horses were advancing troop after troop, squadron after squadron, each wave gaining and consolidating a fresh piece of ground. The group of silent fishermen — if that was what they were — had now been joined by several others. They mostly returned Maeve's friendly greeting and agreed with her in a subdued way that it was, thank God, a grand day.

Maeve revelled in the fresh breakers and found the water less cold than she had expected. In any case she was made for the element and loved the sea in all its moods. Even her body, a strong shapely frame, well-covered, was a swimmer's body. A fine mate for some Celtic Triton, her sister thought, as she watched Maeve splashing about with her kids; and then, looking at the silent watchers down the strand, dismissed the idea of a Celtic Triton as being utterly ridiculous.

Thus the daily visit to the sea became central to the pattern of ensuing days. The weather remained fine and they all agreed — even Hilda — that they were enjoying themselves. They usually brought a picnic lunch with them and watched the waves coming and going as they munched ham sandwiches and crunched chocolate biscuits.

The other group of wave-watchers, the silent and subfusc — 'the abos' as Hilda called them, became as much part of the landscape as the beached hulk of a trawler, the sea wall of the harbour, and the sanderlings along the tide's sibilant rim.

By some miracle (the prayers of Miss Cullen, perhaps) the weather held for the first week of the Rossiter women's visit. During that time Maeve's bereavement was never alluded to and even the little boys, with the sensibility of children — some uncodified law of nature — refrained from talking of their father. Whatever Maeve was feeling she managed to camouflage with her natural gaiety. It was with this quality, which could be interpreted as courage, that she dressed her wound in order to give it time to heal.

But one afternoon going back to the house for tea Maeve decided, as they passed the church, that they should all go in to say a prayer. Like many Catholic churches in Ireland the one at Castlemore had little to recommend it from the outside. It was even less impressive within. There was green mould in the holy water stoup by the door and the interior even lacked the coloured lamps that sometimes alleviate the bad taste of modern iconography. They were rather surprised, therefore, to find so many people quietly seated or kneeling in prayer at an hour when neither Mass nor confession, nor any other advertised service was being heard.

At the sound of the new arrivals those already seated turned round to satisfy their curiosity, and once again the sisters were made to feel that they were intruding upon some private rite rather than making a normal visit to a chapel of the Catholic, Apostolic and Universal Church.

As usual Hilda was the first to comment when they got outside. "They're a weird mob, the Irish. I feel I ought to wear a Member's Badge to get inside that place."

Soon afterwards, returning to Miss Cullen's, they were just passing the field of the junked cars when the swarm of yellow tinker kids rushed out in a state of great excitement. "Missis, missis," two or three of them shouted at the same time, "the first one's after coming in . . . The first one's after coming in!"

Maeve opened her big eyes wide, uncomprehending.

"Yes, missis, the first one's after coming in," yelled a snotty nose who hadn't previously spoken.

"That's right, missis," joined in the chorus.

"The first *what* is just coming in?" asked Hilda with semi-benevolent asperity. The chorus of explanation was instant and incomprehensible. There followed a second or two of silence in which Maeve started laughing at the serious faces confronting her.

"Down on the strand where yez was swimming," explained the eldest itinerant, taking advantage of the pause. "Yes, missis, at the strand," confirmed a girl with scarlet cheeks, obviously snotty-nose's sister.

"Where yez was swimming," said another tow-hair.

"I'm sorry, children, you'll just have to explain," said Maeve and, turning to her own kids, "Do you know what they're talking about, Eamonn?"

"Yes, Mummy."

"What, then?"

"They mean the bodies, Mummy," said Eamonn.

"The bodies? What bodies?"

"The bodies of the two fishermen."

"That were drowned last week in the storm," chipped in Anthony.

"Drowned?"

"The boat turned over."

"And you knew this all the time?" The mother looked from one to the other. The little boys, embarrassed, snatched a furtive look at each other, then blushing, turned to smirk at their tinker pals. Maeve felt a surge of love for their pink faces and for the kindliness of their silence.

"Those people down at the strand must be the families, then?"

"Yes, missis," replied the eldest tinker boy, "but don't be saying I told you."

"Why?" asked Maeve, turning towards the strand.

Now she could see some of the men, bearing between them a heavily-laden blanket, climbing the dunes away from the shore. How easily we could have bumped into it — or it into us, she thought.

"Why do you say not to tell?"

"Miss Harvey and Miss Cullen would kill me, missis."

Maeve wanted to laugh at the little tinker's anxious expression. "And why would Miss Harvey and Miss Cullen kill you?"

"They don't want you to go . . . Aren't you the only tourists left in Castlemore?"

ROBERT BERNEN

The Rush

The rush was the first thing I noticed. The rushes everywhere, through the meadows and grazing lands, clumps and broad areas of blemishes on the fine greenness of the land. "That old blue till," I was told, "that old blue till can never be drained right." That was the cause of the rush, the bluish-grey clay that impacted itself just below the fertile soil and resisted penetration of the surface water to deeper levels. It meant that the land was also a kind of solid lake, a constantly wet mass on which the weeds of wetness thrived. When the weather dried up the ground's condition grew worse. With no deeper level of moisture to draw on the usually soggy clay quickly hardened and cracked. Deprived of rain for a few days the grass ceased its growth. Only the rush retained its foothold and flourished.

So to me the rush appeared only as an ugly weed that was everywhere, and I learned to associate the dark stalk, with its little clump of seed pods on one side near the top, with the wet fields churned into mush by the sharp hooves of lean cattle. A huge part of the back of my own hill was covered in rushes so dense that it was difficult to push through them. I asked an old man whose indeterminate date of birth was somewhere around the beginning of the century how long they had been growing there. "As long as I mind," he told me.

It was all part of the general problem of weeds that preoccupied me constantly in the first years. Weeds grew everywhere, were abundant on what I learned to call my 'park,' those few acres of fenced and green land that some earlier generation of farmers had reclaimed with lime and manure from the coarse heather of the hill to serve as meadow, to yield the mountain hay that was never ready to mow until August, never won until the wet and blustery final weeks of September, the cocks never carried in to be built into a stack until the short, anxious days of October. My eye saw no use in those weeds, saw only blemish. Later I would hear some of the old farmers talking of the worth of those weeds as fodder and questioning the merit of pasture that was limited only to grass itself. Oddly, I discovered, there was almost no weed that some farm animal would not graze. The broad leaves of dock that expanded with terrible rapidity into the after-grass that followed the first — my first — cutting of hay caught my attention and I found out that they were a 'notifiable' weed, by which was meant that it was an offence to have them on your land. By law every farmer was required to spray the dock that grew on his land and so poison it. I wondered if there was another way and was told they could only be dug out, but that the root went very deep and any bit left over would grow again into a full and strong plant. A legend told of the stranger who had appeared at a fair many decades before selling the seeds of a marvellous new plant. Gullible farmers had bought and tried the seed: from it had grown the first dock plants, never again to be eliminated from the green fields. I, fresh to farming, continued to look for a cure.

"Don't worry about them dockens," an old farmer told me, his only literacy his memory of what he had heard from others or himself observed. "When you put your cow out in the morning she'll grab a couple of them dockens, and she'll grab a couple more in the evening when you go to put her in, and there'll be a rich cream on the milk after them. October, this is the month for the dockens."

I found it hard to believe. The dock was a weed, it could hardly enrich the cow's milk. It was, I thought, part of the mechanism of life in the poor hills, to value what you had, lest, despising it, your courage should collapse. Even the weeds were to be respected. But I watched the cow as I put her out and, strangely to me, saw her wrap her long, broad tongue around the first dock leaves she encountered in the morning, chewing them eagerly, then ignoring them until when, as I was told she would, she hastily snatched one or two more on the way home to byre and stall at night. Even odder, I thought, was that the milk did grow richer and creamier. I mentioned the episode to a more modern keeper of cattle on a farm nearer the sea. He listened with open mind. "Now I never would have thought that," he said finally. "The dock is a notifiable weed. I always spray mine." It was the first hint I had of the discontinuity between hill and valley.

If the dock was a useful weed, was in fact fodder, there was no reason to hate it as I had. Digging my vegetable garden later and pondering as I did so the mysterious nature of earth and soil I learned that the dock was indeed the most persistent of plants, that its thick, hard root penetrated and survived at a deeper level than any other, nourishing the broad leaves that shaded and smothered all growing things around. Noticing that its root was the only one that entered into and cracked the hard, rust-coloured layer of infertile clay that lay a foot or so below the surface of the ground I speculated on the possibility that a phase of dock all across the farm would not be the worst thing for the land, that the heavy roots would open it up at a deeper level than any grass could do and so provide a drainage and a path for the roots of the grass itself.

But in the end I found that dock could be controlled by cutting it with a scyth two or three times a year, yielding each time with less resistence to the blade, until it almost disappeared. It was easy to believe that the rush would do so too. My land was full of weeds. I stood looking across the park in perplexity and admiration of their density. That first June when I came up to start the long task of remaking shambles of house and farm in the wetness of almost steady rain I took solace in the chaos and loneliness of the hill from the sudden appearance one morning of yellow irises on the park. Taking my careful steps down the slippery grass of the slope I got a closer look at a large oval patch of stiff sharp leaves in the shape of sword blades. In the middle of the patch a deep hole, and later I would realise that an old piped drain — piped with heavy natural flagstones — had collapsed at that point in its course. The three or four plants that had flowered that morning were what I noticed, rightly conjecturing that fresh cut flowers would reconcile my wife to a large extent to the hardships of our primitive living conditions then. The other flowers that filled the meadow after I had put the sheep off it performed the same task: tiny white daisies, miniature pink wild orchids, buttercups, deep blue hare-bells and others whose names we did not discover. Not far from the wild irises were several equally broad clumps of nettles. Someone passing by while I was looking at them informed me that a load of byre manure had been dumped there for spreading but never had been spread. I found out from my own experience later that thick forests of nettles always developed on unspread manure. One autumn I tried a donkey on the park, letting the sheep and cattle graze it down first and leaving the donkey with the job of cleaning up the remnants. He went to work on the thistles first. I noticed how delicately and carefully he took them into his mouth — was it his lips he was protecting? — and then chewed them up with obvious pleasure. He ignored the iris but went on to the nettles, chewing them into the ground and then pawing up the roots and pulling them out with his front teeth and chewing them up as well. I congratulated myself on this simple success without effort on my part, but in the spring, just when the weather was mending and the fresh grass beginning to grow, the donkey died — the victim of my foolishly transferring him too soon from gentle park to coarse hill grazing — and the nettles, far from defeated, came back with primitive freshness and strength. In the end I found that, like the dock, cutting the nettles and wild yellow irises two or three times in the course of a summer gradually weakened them and let the grass gain a grip around them.

But the rush was different. "Cut them and you'll banish them," I was assured, and on that assurance I wielded my scythe furiously, quixotically against thousands of clumps of rushes. Disappointingly, the rushes always grew again. "I mind the time," a neighbour said, "when you wouldn't find a rush growing anywhere around here for miles." He paused for emphasis and I contemplated the white brush of hair that covered his head, much as the stiff clumps of rushes covered so many acres of the surrounding hill, and wondered how many years before he was thinking of. "Man dear, men were going miles into the hills and carrying back burdens of rushes — a burden of rushes is far heavier nor a burden of corn, you know — to thatch the houses and the byres. You wouldn't get a rush near hand. If you wanted to thatch a stack of hay or one of turf itself you had to go way into the hills for the rushes."

We discussed the matter for a while in similar terms, and then he assured me: "That's the reason there are so many rushes about now. There's no one to cut them, you see."

So the rush could not be banished, only cut, and cut again, over and over, always to return, a permanent guest on the land. Contemplating the image of men climbing far into the hills carrying scythes and stones for cutting the rushes and ropes for binding the cut and gathered rushes into the heavy burdens, then carrying all together the long journey back again, I realised that the rush had not always been unwanted. Adversary in my sense, it was also an ally, a useful weed that provided thatch over everything that was to be protected from the falling rain, and also bedding under animals to keep them from the damp clay floors of their stalls. I remember going to assist at some sheep work one day and admiring the thick clean bed of green rushes that had been prepared in the yard the sheep were to be put into, striking contrast to the muddy dishevelment of my own yard, where I had not yet learned the trick. Finally I heard one of the oldest of the local farmers — a tall thin man in his eighties who never ceased to regret his declining ability to do his own farm work — say that he thought that a good field without rushes wasn't a good field at all.

"I wouldn't have it," he said.

Was it the consolation of the poor farmer, then, on his poor land? There was the story of the blind man who wanted to buy a farm of good land for his son. "Put me on my horse," he said, and the son put him on the horse and then led him down the road. Whenever they came to a farm of land that was for sale the blind man would ask his son whether he saw any rushes. "Yes," the son said at last, after a number of rush-free farms had been left behind. "Hitch my horse to a rush bush." The son did. "This is the farm," the father concluded.

Fighting the weeds I decided at first that it was indeed just that — the consolation of the poor farmer on poor land. Later, when I had lived the life myself for a while, I wondered. Rushes, I learned, were associated with well-limed land and fine friable soil. Where rushes were good crops of oats and potatoes might also grow, or heavy meadows.

But on unfenced, abandoned land near mine I saw that the rushes had spread until they had become like a sea, a dense carpet of smothering stalks that blotted out the grass. And what about the score or more of acres of almost impenetrably thick rushes that grew on the back of my own hill?

"Wait until spring," a near neighbour suggested, "when the real drying comes, and the east wind. Man, the rushes will be as dry as tinder then. Set a match to them and be done with them, and the green grass will grow up after them then." Another neighbour assured me that rushes never burned. To decide, I chose a small isolated clump of rushes near a lake, waited for the dry weather, set the match. A fierce yellow flame flew forth from the first clump and an intense heat, and then as the flame appeared to be dying out it communicated itself suddenly by way of the strands of dry brown grass at the base of the rush to the adjoining clump. As the fire climbed swiftly into the air again I felt the intense heat once more, though only for seconds, and as it was again dying away once more it travelled to the next clump, and so on through the eight or ten clumps of rushes, finally dying out for good.

I tried to imagine the burning of twenty acres of dry rush, imagined the intensity of the heat, wondered about a sudden wind, thought it wise to seek further counsel before striking the irrevocable spark. It was during a break while cutting turf for an old farmer not far from me. The dry weather — the 'winning weather' — had come, and it was time to get the turf cut and set out to dry. We had cut the first floor of a bank of turf not far from his house and were resting then, sitting on the dry heather and looking across over valley and river at the very rushes I had it in mind to burn, and at the new sheep-fence my neighbour and I had just put up between us to keep our flocks separate, its strands of still bright wire gleaming in the warm sun, the still freshly cut posts of larch on which the wire was stretched themselves reflecting the warm light.

"Oh aye," my friend said. "A good idea too, to burn them rushes."

He paused and stuffed his pipe with the morsels of tobacco he had cut and then milled between his rough palms.

"You would be done with them then. A good idea."

He paused again as he struck a wooden match and drew the flame deeply into the briar bowl and over the dry crumbs of tobacco.

"It's a good way to be done with the rushes," he concluded.

I took heart. He was, I knew, a man of much experience in the hills. With his approval I could safely go ahead. I began to visualise the twenty acres freed of rushes putting forth a soft grass manured by the ash itself.

"But what about the man that set a rush fire that time?"

He glanced towards me and away again, drawing deeply on his pipe.

"That time, that was years ago. He had a mind to banish the rushes, you see, and he never told no one. Set the fire one morning and away."

Again he paused and puffed.

"Wait, let me tell you," he resumed. "The fire banished all the rushes, every one. Not a rush left. And then it leapt on to the heather — do you have any heather on that hill? — the heather is very quick to burn, and it burnt all the heather. And then the bog itself itself took fire. It was that dry, the bog itself began to burn, and nothing to stop it. They were out then, man dear the whole countryside was out with spades and shovels, and couldn't stop it. It burnt all before it then, stacks of turf from the year before, that had stood through the winter and no harm come on them, went away in flames, and fences" — he looked at my new fence and then at me — "aye, fences were burnt into the ground, every larch stab, and the wire twisted and rusted after it and useless then. And it took a stack of hay with it, and only it stopped just in time it would take a byre with it next, and the house beside it. Aye!"

He looked squarely at me.

"And the one that set it, he was known. And they could have him for it, too, only they said, enough harm done — he ruined his own land, you see — let him go. But he never made no good after it. No. He never did. And he died soon after."

With the perfect timing of the practised speaker my friend dropped his discourse at that point and never mentioned it again through all the rest of the long day during which we cut and spread his bank of turf, and I myself put the matter from my mind. Later I went to look at the rushes I had burnt and found them growing again fresher and greener than before. So the burning had been a form of pruning, and pruning meant renewal. It was another of the standard themes of Donegal hill talk, the rejuvenating effect of pruning. I heard it said of fish in a lake, or of foxes in a wood that was overrun with them, even of insects. The old farmer reasoned about nature and living things in interlocking chains of being from one thing to another, and when he wanted an animal to die out he left it alone, and when he wanted it to flourish he hunted it, fished it, culled it.

Was the same true of the rushes? Back home I knew I would resort first to poison, to destructive sprays and powders, noxious at times to the sprayers and dusters themselves in spite of their clumsy protective clothes and masks. Some farmers here, too, had tried the sprays, with oddly little success. Success, that is to say, for a year or two, until the deeply hidden remnants of root put forth new and even denser growth. The nature of the land had not been changed by the spray.

A younger farmer, miles away, near the shore, an avid hunter, talked of the culling of foxes. "We shoot them out of the forestries one year, and they're better by far the next. But a few years back, when there was no shootin' in the plantins, they almost died out. Lice, mange, disease, you see, be to finish them nearly."

I wondered if there was no way to eliminate the fox, enemy of lambs, and so of farming and farmers. Strychnine? To which he answered with the parable of the fox that got the strychnine, but when the body rotted a goose from a nearby farm was killed by the same bit of strychnine, and a dog that ate the goose died then. The strychnine never disintegrates, never deteriorates, or returns to the land, he told me. Instead it remains, to kill and kill again.

What answer to all this then, I wondered?

"Nature," he said. "Nature. All things must live, and we will live among them. Leave the foxes alone. Nature will keep the balance."

I followed the direction of his thinking then when I looked at the rushes, at the sea of rushes that choked broad acreages on the back of the hill. Leave them alone, let them flourish to the point of death. And what about the grass? Was not the grass an ally? And the heather? If the sheep that steadily cropped the grass and heather were kept from that stretch of hill for six months of the year, the six months when grass and heather grow best, would they, the grass and the heather, not fight the rush? Would they not drain the land with strengthened, ever deeper roots, sucking up more and more of the moisture, drying the land, pushing out the rush, robbing it of the wetness it could not live without? It was worth trying. But it was slow, a project of years, not one season, a long, slow, patient process, not as swift as poison, not as easy. It meant letting the living herbage strike its own balance, amend the condition of the land itself, in its own slow way. But it would be without poison, and it would be more lasting, until the next uncontrolled invasion of the sheep.

In time, slowly, I saw the change develop, year by year, the grass and the heather dry the land, extend their area bit by bit, invade the heart of the fading withering rushes. Broad areas of rushes, where once neither I nor any sheep could walk, thinned out, weakened, failing, leaving the ground for the grass, until finally, when they had given ground enough, I too wondered whether I wanted them all entirely banished from my land. In heavy winter snows I saw the hungering sheep live for days on the green tips of the rushes and, as the snow receded, on the heavy grass trapped and dried at the root, a natural winter hay, a natural life saving provision.

No wonder the poor farmer of the hill did not despise the rush, did not see it, as I saw it, as his enemy. For he saw nothing as his enemy, not rush, or dock, or thistle, or nettle, or any weed, and not the foxes either and the swarming rabbits that I so hated, but saw all things as part of an interlocking chain and cycle and harmony. It was, I saw at last, more than the consolation of the poor farmer. It was part of his understanding of the way things really are. The rush that thatched his house and byre and stacks of hay and corn and turf, that bedded his animals, and often foddered them in winter — it too was life. The symbol, possibly of life, when, every first day of February, he wove it strandwise with his hands into a simple Brigid's cross and presented himself at his neighbour's door, and carried into the house the cross of fresh green rushes chanting an old formula that he would never question: *sheh baha, sheh baha, sheh baha* — it is life, it is life, it is life.

WOLF MANKOWITZ

The Bard of Ballyelohesra

Jackson Sweetman is a Man of Letters, of an age as indeterminate as the number of Irish whiskeys he has consumed in the process of telling the literary historical version of this story.

Of course, Sweetman's oracular West British vocalising will be familiar to RTE listeners who follow the adventures of those old gentlemen who seem to have haunted every rural spot where the great W.B. Yeats spotted a fairy; or were on the corner of every mean street, entering or leaving the local watering-place, as James Joyce shuffled by and tripped over a minor poet or a fluxing cat. Jackson Sweetman fortunately has seen it all, and now, in his later years, lives off it, poorly. But drinks off it tolerably well.

Thus it will come as no surprise to RTE literary talks' listeners to hear Sweetman speak of the grand and moving ceremony of the scattering of the ashes of that greatest of almost unknown Cork poets Tagh O'Muirtagh. In accordance with his wish frequently expressed in the pubs of Kilburn, they were strewn to the winds in the heathered hills of Ballyelohesra in South West Cork. It goes without saying that, apart from Mrs. O'Muirtagh, the only person present at the simple ceremony was the poet's friend and drinking partner, that well-known Man of Letters, Jackson Sweetman. Reduced to the duration of about four large doubles without water (Sweetman agreeing with W. C. Fields about what fish do in it), the facts, however, are as follows.

Jackson Sweetman was coming out of Bush House above Fleet Street in London Town when he observed Tagh O'Muirtagh bullfighting with a red bus. Sweetman had been recording reminiscences of Yeats and Joyce for listeners in Pakistan. He was a little parched and dry from the effort but it was immediately obvious to him that Tagh had found a source of drink. By the time the nimble poet had missed the third red bus Sweetman had decided to suffer being out-talked by his garrulous countryman, only provided he had the price of a few pints. This Tagh had and much more as it turned out, for he had that very morning been paid by an advertising agency who were using his charming quatrains on its client's toilet paper.

O'Muirtagh was triumphant. "May it give them piles!" he

exclaimed. "Come and have a drink, you old bollox!" Jackson agreed, reeling in the delectable fumes of whiskey and nicotine which issued from the poet like sulphurous vapours from a volcano mouth.

Can there be a better place in the world for a minor poet to drop dead than the pavement outside El Vino's, a pub which has scarred the livers of more scribblers than Jackson Sweetman has swallowed warm Bushmills? The sympathetic journalists flooded out of the famous pub and rallied round the prostrate poetaster. Through their good offices Sweetman was able to arrange for Tagh's corpse to be quietly reduced to ashes at the Golders Green crematorium ten minutes before a wealthy Kosher butcher. Unfortunately Fleet Street's tribute didn't run to a dignified urn but Sweetman, (who was extremely partial to Molly Malone Irish Whiskey Tinned Fruit Cake which he brought over with him on his occasional visits to London, for it saved wasting money on food), produced an empty tin. Tagh's ashes barely filled it. Over the fruit cake tin Sweetman intoned a few inapproprite lines from Yeats' Easter poem, and set out for his BBC-financed return journey to Dublin.

But such is the determined loyalty drinkers show towards one another that Sweetman insisted he be despatched via the Swansea-Cork ferry; for he well knew O'Muirtagh's desire to be strewn to the winds of Ballyelohesra. As the poet had written:

I will arise and go sir
To the hills of Ballyelohesra,
Where the small wind through the heather
Will make my old bones feel bedder.

On the ferry-boat Sweetman found a middle-aged German property dealer of dubious sex who seemed to enjoy paying for whiskey while he intoned such verses. Eventually the bearded lady said, "I am luffing to hear your Irish-speak. Can you please in English now speak me one *volkisch* poem?"

Whereupon Sweetman drained his glass, fixed the Teutonic creature with the dead eye of a week-old pollock and weaved his way carefully to the gents.

On this occasion he left his Molly Malone Fruit Cake tin on

the bar. He had previously left it in several bars in London, the bar of the British Railways Swansea Special, and in two Welsh bars; and yet so powerful are the webs of friendship that Tagh followed him out on every occasion in the hands of some acolyte drinking companion. In the last case Sweetman was battling with his fly-buttons as the German thing accosted him in the door of the gents.

"You haff ofer-looked somsing I think, no?" she said mischievously.

Sweetman swivelled his dead pollock eye down towards his flies, but all was in perfect order.

"Your Molly Maloney." The Teuton offered him the tin with a coy smile.

"*Danke schön gnadige Frau,*" Sweetman intoned.

"*Frau*? Ach no, I am still free," she giggled invitingly, pulling her thin moustache.

Waiting for a friendly shebeen to open Sweetman left the Molly Malone tin on the kerb of a Cork city quay for a moment while he attacked the door furiously. Returning, he was just in time to prevent an urchin from prising it open with the horse's-hoof stone-extractor on his penknife.

"Away with you spalpeen," Sweetman intoned. "Never fear, O'Muirtagh," he said fervently to the tin, "you are safe with me."

So it was that, after a long bus journey in the course of which several passengers cheered when Sweetman, holding up the Molly Malone tin, intoned O'Muirtagh's poem on the Great Bank Strike with its unforgettable refrain:

For many a glass we drank those months
When rubber cheques were as good as punts
And poets were happy as a tinker's tyke,
God give us soon another bank strike!

Finally Sweetman was dropped off with a near-empty Bushmills bottle and the battered tin in the centre of the village of Ballyelohesra. He observed the silent garish multicoloured houses and shops all closed, apparently to celebrate a festival which was proclaimed on a hand-written banner bedecked with two strings of damp motheaten bunting. He tracked through the giant confetti of Tayto crisp packets with which all local fiestas were celebrated, and stumbled into the Elohesra Bar. There a pale, exhausted woman attended by six tiny children all between the ages of two and three, swept up a small hillock of fag ends, bottle-tops, crunched crisps, fragments of partly digested food and shattered pool balls.

"The pub-singing contest isn't until tonight," the woman said "if you're a pub-singer." But under Sweetman's expert persuasion this unpromising opening was warmed by a grubby glass containing a generous shot of the necessary, and a confusing account of where in the hills above could be found the O'Muirtagh cottage.

"He was a great man," Sweetman sighed chestily as he downed the drop.

"An actor, wasn't he?" the woman said.

"Poet," replied Sweetman.

"Sure isn't it the same thing." She extracted a small child from the heap of fag-ends and dusted it with a couple of sharp slaps on its bare posterior.

Sweetman invested the larger part of his remaining cash resources in a small bottle of Paddy, and set out bearing the Molly Malone tin under his arm, up the mile long boreen which led steeply to the thin fields below the common bogland in the heights of the Elohesra Hills. As he approached the picturesque waterless and electricity-free grimy white cottage, a brown, worn-looking woman came out of a tiny stony field bearing a pair of buckets of milk. She glared at the parched stranger resting breathless upon a rock, a small empty whiskey bottle in his hand and a cake tin on his lap.

"Would it be Mrs. O'Muirtagh?" Sweetman coughed.

"It might be," the woman replied, squinting suspiciously.

He rattled the tin at her triumphantly. "God bless you, madam!" he proclaimed, getting to his feet and bowing in his most gracious Man of Letters mode. "I bear you from foreign parts a token of your great husband."

The woman put down the two pails slowly and studied first Sweetman, and then the profered tin. "Ten years he's been away," she said, as to herself.

"His spirit was always here," Sweetman assured her. "I wonder madam, would you have in the house a drop of the stuff? It's a long walk for an ageing man of letters."

"His spirit was here, was it?" she asked him.

"It was, it was" Sweetman assured her.

"And what about the rest of him?" Mrs. O'Muirtagh asked, turning upon Sweetman the dark baleful glare in which mountain women specialise.

Sweetman sighed. "Like all of us, he was a slave to his muse." He again offered her the cake tin.

"Ten years I'm waiting here with him galleylumping all over the world with his bloody muse or any other woman he can get his hands on," she said like thunder rumbling in the distant hills.

"His heart was ever true," intoned Sweetman. "Would you, I wonder, have in the house a drop of anything at all, at all?"

Mrs. O'Muirtagh took the tin from him and carried it to the precipitous edge of the path. "Ten years away and all he sends me is a bloody fruit cake! The drunken fecker! Well he knew I never eat the stuff," she exclaimed. She threw the tin like a Gaelic football into the rocky abyss below.

And so, as the fruit cake tin split on the rocks below, the ashes of the poet Tagh O'Muirtagh were, as that well-known Man of Letters, Jackson Sweetman, will be telling us this coming Sunday on RTE, scattered to the winds of the heathered mountains he loved as much as any poet can be expected to love an area in which there are very, very few poetry-lovers left.

NEIL BOYD

Jacob

A late autumn evening, and the vast unheated church in London's East End was as cold as a barn.

At the back, a solitary sixty-watt bulb, without a shade, barely lit up the exit. On the sanctuary, suspended from an invisible chain, a red lamp glowed before the tabernacle.

There was one other source of light. Near the Lady Altar, a circle of quivering candles burned before the Virgin's statue. An old gentleman was seated beside the candles, facing the sanctuary, his hands across his temples, his bony fingers covering his eyes. A walking stick, a pair of knitted gloves and a Homburg hat were on the bench beside him.

At 6.30, a clock sounded metallically in the sacristy. Soon afterwards, an inner door connecting the sacristy to the presbytery opened. The sound of it made the old man sit bolt upright and put on his spectacles.

A tall priest appeared carrying a bunch of large keys. He walked down the side aisle to the Lady Altar peering about him as he went. He noticed the stranger sitting on the bench.

"Did you light those candles?"

"Yes, Father."

The priest noticed a slight pause between the words. "All of them?"

"Yes."

"Have you a special intention to pray for that you lit all those?" The priest sounded kind and reassuring.

"For my wife," the old man said, his voice breaking.

The priest could not tell if he was upset or simply very old. Nor could he place the accent. It was London, almost cockney, but with a difference. The consonants were clipped so that he wondered if the man was from South Africa.

"She's not sick, I hope."

"No, Father." The same slight pause. Then, as if summoning up his courage: "I've come especially from Earl's Court to speak to you about my wife. You see, I'm a Jew and she's not happy with me."

"You think I can help?" the priest said. "Stay here a little minute till I lock the church. One of my curates should have done it half an hour ago but he's slow as a wet week."

The Jew was thinking, I was lucky, then.

The priest went to the end of the church where he looked

into the confessionals, then made his way into the semi-circle of light before disappearing into the drafty porch. An iron key grated in the lock, a rusty bolt was drawn, then another. The sixty-watt bulb was extinguished.

When the priest returned, the stranger was on his feet.

"I'll have to blow the candles out at present, in case of fire, but rest assured I'll light them first thing in the morning before Mass begins. Now, if you'd care to come with me."

The priest waited for the Jew to gather up his belongings before blowing the candles out in one mighty puff.

Guided by the priest's pocket torch they walked towards the sacristy. The Jew was saying as he shuffled along: "I like the lighting of candles. For the Sabbath, Father. My wife told me if I lit a lot of candles for her before the Virgin's statue my prayers would be answered. She was right. I did put money in the box, of course."

The general uncomfortableness of the priest's study was something the stranger noticed at once. No fond woman had been let loose here. The patterened carpet was threadbare, the glass shade of the table lamp cracked, the ceiling yellow with cobwebs in the corners. But the shelves were full of books, a fact which the old Jew appreciated.

Away from the gloom of the church, they were able to look at each other.

"My name is Fr. Moore. I'm parish priest here."

"I saw your name at the back of the church, Father. You call it a confessional, I think."

"Indeed. And may I know your name?"

"Mr. Broder."

They shook hands. Fr. Moore, approaching fifty, with a shock of black, greying hair, noticed that Mr. Broder's bony, rope-like hand was trembling.

He helped his visitor out of his black, heavy almost ankle-length overcoat that smelt powerfully of mothballs and hung it on a hook behind the door. He put the hat on his desk, the stick in a corner.

He gestured to a covered, green armchair. "Please make yourself comfortable. It's a cold evening altogether. I'll just light the fire."

Before bending down to light the gas, Fr. Moore had time

to notice the Jew's milky, seal-like eyes above the horn-rimmed spectacles. These were perched on the end of his very Jewish nose. He was dressed smartly in a dark grey suit of excellent quality with waistcoat to match. The priest tried to guess the age of this benign-looking old fellow, and wondered why his wife was unhappy with him.

As the priest rubbed his hands and sat down on an easy chair opposite him, Mr. Broder said, "I put seventy five pence in the box for the candles. I hope that was enough."

"Exceedingly generous of you."

"I'm glad," Mr. Broder said. He was sitting on the edge of his chair as if not wanting to take up too much room.

"Now, about your problem."

"It's not my problem. It's a spiritual problem."

"Your wife's?"

"Yes."

The old man's top dentures tended to drop on to the lower with a click. This happened when he puffed out his cheeks as though blowing on cold, invisible fingers in front of his face. Dear God, Fr. Moore thought, he must be very old. He said: "Is your wife elderly?"

"No, she's only sixty-four." Mr. Broder rubbed his right eye over the top of his glasses. "I'm eighty-three."

"The years have been as kind as a mother to you."

Mr. Broder exhaled noisily. "My wife is threatening to leave me."

"I'm very sorry to hear it." To himself, Fr. Moore said, Not for another man, surely?

"You see, Father, my wife thinks she's not married to me."

"Why does she think that?"

"Because we were married in the register office."

Fr. Moore nodded a couple of times. "You were not married in the Catholic Church and your wife is a Catholic."

"I forgot to tell you that."

"I guessed. Perhaps you had objections on religious grounds?"

"It wasn't that. I'm a Jew but not much of one. No, it was because I'd been married before."

"How long have you been married to your present wife?"

"For thirty wonderful years. And before that, so I keep

nothing from you, for another ten."

"Now she is talking about leaving you."

"She is Irish, you see, Father. Like yourself." Mr. Broder's eyes were watering so much he had to remove his glasses and mop up. "Bridget O'Driscoll before I married her. From Cork. All her relatives are priests and nuns."

"It's a wonder Bridget managed to get born at all."

The old man didn't seem to hear. "Lately, over the last few years at any rate, she's been accusing me of enticing her away from her religion when she was a young girl. Sometimes she speaks of suicide." He sniffed and swallowed painfully. "Mostly of murder."

"Who is she threatening to murder?"

"Me."

"You are exaggerating, Mr. Broder, surely. Or perhaps your wife is disturbed."

"I mean she threatens to leave me, Father. That would kill me off as quickly as if she put poison in my tea. Your religion doesn't encourage murder, Father, does it?"

Fr. Moore, smiling, shook his head.

"I say to her, 'Bridie, I'm over eighty. Without you, I'd crawl into a hole like an animal and die.' That would be a worse sin than her marrying me in the first place, Father, wouldn't it?"

"Oh, indeed, it would."

" 'If you left me, Bridie,' I say, 'who would do for me all the things the Law forbids me to do for myself on the Sabbath? I'm already a good age for a corpse. Don't push me into my grave before my time.' " As if to emphasise that his time was not far off: "I got over two major operations recently, Father. I had my gall bladder out and I had that prostate operation, too."

Seeing the old man about to dissolve into tears, the priest put in, "What made you come all this way, Mr. Broder? Earl's Court is the other side of town."

Mr. Broder composed himself. He explained that he and his wife had visited friends in Bethnal Green a couple of months before. It was a Sunday. "I came with my wife to your church, I often go to Mass with her, and you preached a sermon we both liked very much."

"That is kind of you."

"If you'll pardon the liberty, you told a very Jewish story. About a Pharisee and a tax collector. And you said that the Pharisee who kept all the laws was a sinner and the tax collector who broke all the laws was really very good inside."

Fr. Moore kept a straight face. "It *was* a Jewish story, all right."

"You said, this proves we can never judge what people are really like. You even took the example of Catholics marrying . . ."

"Outside the Church."

"Yes. They may have broken the law but no one should criticise because only God sees the heart. The tax collector probably had to go back to his tax collecting to keep his wife and kiddies. Likewise, you said, many people married outside the Church have to stay with their families because they can't walk out on their obligations, either. But God has His big eyes of mercy on them always."

"You have a grand memory and no mistake."

"It lodged in my brain like a bullet. My wife and I have spoken about that sermon a hundred times. I said to her, 'You see, Bridie, we've got to stay together. Your Jesus says so.' She replies, 'But we have no children.' 'Aren't I old and helpless enough to count as a child?' I say. She doesn't know the answer to that. She just keeps quiet so she can't lose and I can't win."

"So you came to me."

"I knew there are always two Catholic priests who would understand me, Pope John and Fr. Moore. And Pope John is dead."

"You flatter me," the priest said. "Tell me a bit more about yourself. When, for instance, were you first married?"

"First I was yoked to the ox in a synagogue in Dalston in 1920. Terrible? I can't tell you. I had one son. He's married in Perth, Australia. He had to move into another continent to get away from her. No farther can he go till they charter flights to the moon."

"What was the trouble?"

"What wasn't the trouble? The Jewish Bible says a wife's arguing is like the dripping of rain. I tell you that woman could have worn away Mount Zion."

"Did you live long together?"

"According to the calendar, only eighteen years. By that time I was so run down I caught TB. The fresh air complained at of having to go in my lungs. It came out condensed like coal. I went to a sanatorium across the River."

"A sanatorium?"

"That's what they called them in those days. It was a low building with fresh air running in all directions like a Jew in search of business. For two years I was there. They collapsed one lung at a time and filled me up with little balls so I felt like a bag of popcorn."

"A desperate existence," the priest said sympathetically.

"The four walls got bored looking at me. Every time my wife visited me I had a relapse."

"She came frequently?"

"Every week. She said it was her duty. It made her miserable so she was happy. At least I had six Sabbath days rest from her each week."

"Is this where you met Bridget?"

"I'm coming to that. When I was moved on to the verandah I began to improve. Because this was when Bridie was posted to our ward as a nurse, and suddenly the four great rivers flowed again in paradise. A vulture had been picking at my innards for eighteen years, so think what it was like to be looked after by someone as light and soft as a seagull. That's how my Bridie looked to me in those days in her uniform."

"When you got better you didn't go back to your wife. Your first wife, I mean."

"One Daniel is enough for us Jews, Father. I said to the present Mrs. Broder, 'Bridie,' I said, 'God must've had a lapse of memory. He sent me a piece of good luck.' 'And what might that be?' she said in her lovely brogue. She had only left Cork two years before but she sounds no different today. 'You,' I said. 'But you're married already. I can't be living with you,' she said."

"But she did?"

The old Jew bowed his head and shrugged. "We were young, in love. And after being together every day for eighteen months in the sanatorium, we couldn't bear to. . . ." His voice trailed off.

"Your first wife divorced you, I suppose."

"Not at first. I didn't put any pressure on her because Bridie said she would never marry me anyway since the Pope wouldn't let her. I said to her, 'Who is this Pope? He's not Moses, is he?' But she insisted, 'He is bigger altogether than Moses.' 'How can he be bigger than Moses? Didn't God give Moses the ten commandments?' Bridie said, 'And wasn't one of them, Thou shalt not commit adultery?' Father, I tell you, Moses I could deal with. Didn't Moses himself marry more than once and, my Rabbi say, two Gentile women besides? But Moses and the Pope together was too much for me."

"So, I understand, you lived together unmarried."

Mr. Broder looked up. "We didn't please either of these infallible gentlemen, as my wife calls them."

"It seems not."

"Six years after my divorce, I said to my Bridie, 'What about it this time?' And she said, 'I will. I dare say Almighty God won't recognise the face on me at the register office after all these years.' We got married in Chelsea. The happiest day of my life."

The old man sat back in his chair beaming seraphically, resting his bald head.

"I gather from what you say that your first wife is still—"

"She is, Father."

"She must be quite advanced in years."

"I don't begrudge her the blessing of long life. She never married again. But each year I rush to get a new telephone directory to see if her name has dropped out of it. But it's always there, stinging my eyes."

"Maybe she died and her name's not been taken out of the book yet."

"What can I do, Father, write and ask her if she's still alive? Jews are a little bit suspicious. She may think I'm after her money."

Fr. Moore stooped to turn down the gas. The room was becoming hot. "Am I the first priest you have discussed this with?"

"No. Four years ago, I discussed it briefly with a priest. My wife attends his church most Sundays."

"You went for thirty-six years without consulting a priest?"

"Well, you see, Father, my Bridie says she knows the laws of her Church better than I know the *Shema*! And I've never been fond of Catholic priests. Besides, I wouldn't like my Rabbi to look on me as a Goy-chaser. I don't even tell him I go to church with my wife."

"I understand."

"You know how it is, Father. My Rabbi always tells us, the first Christians like John and Paul were great Jew-haters, and there'll always be anti-Semitism while the New Testament is read. That's what he says."

"Does he, now. Very interesting."

"He's like you, so learned he uses books for wall paper. And he's sharp. Is he sharp! Why, I tell you, with his knowledge of the Talmud he can split hairs faster than a barber can cut them."

Fr. Moore laughed aloud. "When you spoke to the priest, what did he have to say?"

"That while my first wife is still alive we would never be able to marry as my wife wishes, and that in the eyes of the Church we are living in sin. He said, 'It's not my law, Mr. Broder.' 'I know,' I said, 'it's the Pope's.' He answered, 'No, it's God's law. The Pope didn't make it so he can't change it.' "

Fr. Moore nodded his agreement with his brother priest.

Mr. Broder said, "We Jews don't like divorce, either, but we don't make laws about it and say, 'God doesn't allow this or that.' "

"This priest you talked with, did he have nothing helpful to suggest?"

"He said, and I remember it word for word, 'Ours is not a vindictive religion, Mr. Broder. If your wife is dying you can always call me or any other priest and one of us will come and administer the last rites.' "

Fr. Moore saw clouds of sorrow sitting on the old Jew's shoulder. "What did you think of that?"

"That the voice was the voice of Jacob but the hands were the hands of Esau. My poor wife, when she heard this, went out to buy all the things a priest needs when he administers the last rites: candlesticks, candles like the ones I lighted in your church, white linen cloths and a crucifix that stands up straight on the table."

"That was an unnecessary expense."

"Now my wife keeps these things in a drawer next to our bed. She kneels down every night and I can see her picturing herself on the point of death and wondering whether the priest will get to her in time and what will happen if he doesn't. And she doesn't sleep, in case she dies sleeping and nobody knows. And my heart is ready to burst with all the sadness in it." With the back of his hand he wiped his brow. "Because she is right, you see, I did draw her away from her religion, so I'm to blame for all her misery."

Fr. Moore said nothing. He sighed deeply.

"I'm making her more miserable than my first wife made me. But I'm too old, Father, to do without her now. I thought when I was young, old people had no need of women. But I need my Bridie if I'm to draw a single breath."

Fr. Moore said, "It really is true, our religion tries not to be vindictive, Mr. Broder. But I'd like to think your wife has a happy life as well as the hope of a happy death."

The old Jew screwed up his eyes and nodded his head with all the energy he could muster.

"It would be sad," Fr. Moore went on, "if Mrs. Broder should find, not joy but at least relief when you pass away because she can practise her religion again."

"What can I do, Father? Tell me, please. I'll do anything, go anywhere, give away my last penny if only we can stay together and she can be happy. I believe things can get fixed up in Rome sometimes. The rich people, the really rich, I mean, can get a divorce, can't they? I read about it once in *The Jewish Chronicle.*"

"I assure you," the priest answered gently, "money and influence are not the answer. All the cases are discussed impartially and with perfect justice."

"Oh, Father," Mr. Broder said, "I didn't come for justice. I came for mercy."

Fr. Moore pursed his lips and nodded.

"We all worship the same God of compassion, Father. Don't we all look on Him as *Ovenu Malkinu,* our Father, our

King?"

"Indeed we do, Mr. Broder, but since your first wife is still alive and the bond between you remains—"

"How can there be a bond between us," the old Jew snorted. "I haven't seen her in forty years. I don't know if she has black hair or grey, if she still drips like a broken rain-gutter or is deaf and dumb as a post. I haven't thought of her for forty years except to thank God I am rid of her and living in paradise. And," he added, "she has probably the same feelings about me." His voice was strident now. "How can there be a bond between two total strangers?"

"With the deepest respect, Mr. Broder, we have to sort things out in a way your wife understands and approves."

"I beg your pardon," the old man said, wiping his eyes and polishing the lenses of his glasses with an enormous starched white handkerchief. "White," he said proudly. "My Bridie."

"I was going to say that while your first wife is still alive there is one way out of the dilemma."

"I can't, Father."

The priest was puzzled. "Can't what?"

"That other priest said I could become a Christian."

Fr. Moore tried to intervene without success.

"Father, I'm a Jew, a shabby little Jew. I worship in a shabby broken-down synagogue and we have a shabby worship to go with it. Everything is shabby. Every Friday evening, I read the eighteen benedictions. Before I've hardly begun, everybody else is finished. They speak so fast God Himself can't keep up."

Fr. Moore just managed to get in, "We have prayers like that in the Catholic Church."

"But in spite of everything, Father, I'm a Jew. How could I become a Gentile? Can I leave my kin and my skin?"

"But, Mr. Broder—"

"No use, Father. I never asked my Bridie to turn Jewish even in the years she never went to church."

Fr. Moore waited for the storm to die down. Then, quietly: "Not for one moment did I think of asking you to be baptised. And that is the blessed truth."

"But you said—"

"That there is one way out of your dilemma."

"And it's got nothing to do with becoming a Christian?"

"Nothing at all, I swear."

The Jew lifted his head. "Forgive an old fool, Father."

"You and your wife. . . ." The priest hesitated. "You can live as brother and sister, as the Church's lawyers put it."

The Jew looked crestfallen. "Then there's no hope for us."

It was Fr. Moore's turn to look downcrest and bewildered. Was this old man, together with his aging wife, so attached to the pleasures of the flesh? He scarcely looked able for it.

Mr. Broder said, "We *have* lived as brother and sister, as you call it, for eight years now, ever since my wife had her hysterectomy."

The priest suddenly understood. "Your wife may not know the Church's law quite as well as you know the *Shema,* after all. For the last eight years, she was perfectly entitled to return to the sacraments."

The old Jew's eyes were stretched wide.

"Did you mention this to your wife's parish priest when you spoke to him?"

"It hardly seemed delicate. I didn't know that your Church is so interested in—"

"That accounts for it."

"Mrs. Broder and I have for eight years kept ourselves pure for the day of her return to the holiness of her Church."

"And you did not know that that fact alone—" The old Jew had grasped the point.

After a while, Mr. Broder asked, "Will we be allowed to sleep in the same room?"

"Of course. Just go on as before."

"My wife, will she believe me when I tell her?"

"I'll write her a note if you like."

"Please, Father. She'll believe what a priest says."

Fr. Moore went to his desk while Mr. Broder, almost beside himself with joy, was breathing quickly and clicking his dentures like billiard balls.

"You know what our Bible says, Father. The wife is a man's rib. Isn't that good? His rib."

In a not very clear script, the priest wrote:

Dear Mrs. Broder,

Greetings in God and St. Patrick.

I have been talking to Mr. Broder. We have got on very well together. He has told me about the problem which has caused you so much sadness over the years.

In view of the circumstances, I do not think it is a difficult problem to solve. Mr. Broder tells me you have been living as "brother and sister" for some time. That is all the Church requires. I will write to the Bishop immediately and soon I hope to hear your confession and give you Holy Communion.

You have had some unhappy years but I believe you have not been separated from God. In your heart, where it really matters, you were always with Him. Your husband has told me how you have continued going regularly to Sunday Mass.

I have told Mr. Broder that you cannot go through a form of Catholic marriage while his first wife is still alive. But that is no reason for you to separate. On the contrary, you have lived with Mr. Broder for so long and loved him so well since the time he was first unwell that it cannot be God's will for you to part from each other now. You would be lost and lonely without each other. Just go on *exactly* as you have gone on over the past eight years. Mr. Broder will explain what I mean by this.

This is the time of Advent. I am happy to be able to bring you tidings of great joy. I hope to meet you within a week so that everything may be well.

Pray quietly within your heart and you will find peace. May the God of peace give you unending peace.

The priest signed his name: (Fr.) Seamus Moore.

All the time the priest was writing, the old Jew kept his eyes on him. Fr. Moore saw those eyes when eventually he raised his head from the page. He smiled at him and Mr. Broder smiled back.

"Father, now I know why Jesus has so many disciples."

"Why is that?"

"He must have been like you."

"Believe me, Mr. Broder, what I am doing for you any Catholic priest in the whole world could have done equally well."

"Except for one thing, Father."

"What is that?"

"Only you were able to convince me that you could solve our problem."

"It's kind of you to say so."

"Today the waters are divided," Mr. Broder said. "Today I have caught a glimpse of heaven."

Fr. Moore put the letter in an envelope without sealing it. Handing it to Mr. Broder, he said, "There are just one or two details I'd like to take down. I have to inform the Bishop, you see, also the parish priest where your wife goes to Mass. Otherwise he might be surprised to see her come to the altar rails at the time of Communion."

"Certainly, Father. What would you like to know?"

Fr. Moore, his pen poised above his note paper, had a momentary lapse. "Could you tell me, first, your Christian name?"

"Jacob," he said.

ERIK HAUGAARD

A Decent Man

The rain was not soft, it came down as if it were rehearsing for a new flood. The water and the oncoming darkness obscured the view of the houses across the street. I wondered, if I had been Noah, what animals I would have taken along — I could think of a few I would have left behind. I turned from watching through the window this wash-day of the Lord, to contemplate the bottles, lined on shelves behind the bar. I was draining my glass of beer, wishing I had more taste for it, when the door was thrown open; and for a moment the wind and rain entered, with the new customer, the quiet room.

The newcomer nodded twice: once for me and once for the woman behind the counter; there was no one else in the bar. Then looking around at all the empty stools, he carefully chose the one next to mine. "He wants to talk," I thought, and debated in my mind whether to be annoyed or not. Not to need to talk can make a wise man of a fool. Keeping yourself to yourself you can sit like a Buddha on a throne.

"What would you be drinking?" the stranger looked at my empty glass.

I thought of saying, 'Nothing, I am leaving now. Got to get home.' But the weather outside and the wish for an ear that would listen, which I spied in the man's eyes, made me say instead, "A glass of lager."

"A pint of stout and a pint of lager," he shouted gaily.

The woman, in turn, repeated his order; but gave him a sour look, as if she knew him well and had little use for him.

'What ever he is going to tell, she has heard it before,' I thought. 'She thinks him a poor sort of fellow, not worthy of a smile.'

"The fields will be flooding soon." I judged my companion to be a farmer, and decided out of courtesy to talk about crops or the sale of sheep.

"Aye, and there is more where it is coming from." He glanced at his glass as if he did not care how much or little it rained; yet he said politely, "When it is this time of year and she blows from northwest, it may never stop."

I smiled, I knew the Irish weather. Taking a sip from my beer, I was wondering what to say next, when he asked me where I came from and if I was a visitor here.

While I answered, in words I knew by heart, I asked myself

whether I had not been a visitor all my life, wherever I had lived — even in my own country.

"They are farmers, too." It wasn't as much a question as a statement of fact. "It isn't much of a life."

I wanted to protest, for Danish farmers are rich; but he didn't give me a chance, he had more important things that needed to be said.

"I have two brothers that are priests." He nodded his head as if he were counting them. "But I did better in school than they." This he said in a slow, measured way, as if it were some truth dug up from deep underground and kept. "But I wouldn't have made much of a priest." He grinned and waited for me to protest.

"It is a call," I mumbled, hoping the phrase would not offend.

"For some," he said merrily, and I knew that his brothers — at least in his eyes — were not among them. "My father was a very decent man but hard." He frowned. "Hard as the rocks in the field."

There was nothing for me to say. I noticed that his glass was empty and I beckoned to the woman, who was sitting at the very end of the bar, as far away as she could get. She stood up slowly as if she didn't want to come. My glass was still half-full; I drank some and ordered another for myself as well. As she drew the pint of stout, being careful to give it neither too much nor too little head, she glanced for a second at my companion, and I knew she thought him a fool.

"A very decent man, but hard." Just as the woman was setting the glasses in front of us, he repeated the words; and she answered, as if it were a play and she had a line to speak.

"But he is dead!"

"Aye, God rest his soul," my companion said, and wrinkled his brow either in sorrow or hate. "But he was hard, Mary."

The woman gave me my change, as if she had not heard him, and returned to her lonely stool. He lifted his glass. His hands were broad from toil. I let my gaze rest on his clothes; his black jacket had spots on the lapels and was too tight under the arms. It was his best suit, I am sure, and told the world that he was poor.

"A man can only take so much, then something breaks."

While he spoke, he did not look at me, but at the woman at the end of the bar. She stared at some point in the air; and I thought, "It is on purpose, she is seeing nothing there."

"Jaysus, it's a mucky place." He grinned and waved his hand to take in the town, sotted with rain. "What made you stop here?"

"A tyre blew out, they are fixing it at the garage." I smiled, for he was right. It was the kind of village that you drove through. Yet to them it was the centre of the world.

"I would like to have gone . . ." he paused for a moment, then added, "somewhere else."

"Where?" I asked, for somewhere else, is that not where we all long to be.

"Far away," he smiled broadly, "like the South Seas."

The woman at the end of the counter laughed, as if the thought of a farmer in County Kerry wishing for islands where palms mirrored themselves in blue lagoons were absurd.

"I would like to go there, too." I sipped my pint; his was almost gone. I had spoken a lie, for those islands are best not visited. Once there, behind their coral reefs, you cannot dream of them again. It sobered Jack London enough for him to kill himself.

"I never had a chance," he whispered, while beckoning the woman to fill our glasses.

I hated him for having said those words, the most unworthy any mouth can utter. "My tyre must be fixed," I mumbled. Now I wanted to leave.

"There's plenty of time," he said and pushed our glasses towards the woman's hands. She looked questioningly at me; and when I nodded, she smiled as if we were conspirators, and I thought, 'She hates him but loves him, too.'

"Everyone has had their chance." While I spoke I kept my gaze on the man to see if the words would hurt.

"Aye, that is the worst of it." He smiled and his smile was a little like a child's. "And what would you be doing here?" He moved his hand a little and I knew what he meant, for that slight gesture took in all of Ireland.

"I am a writer." I had thought of saying I was a poet; but for this man it would not do. He had had too many dreams himself, and dreams wear a man into a shadow.

"And they pay you for that." He winked. "I know, there's one living near here. He bought a big house. There is no end to his money."

I grinned and let him believe that there was no end to mine as well, for I knew that every shilling he had earned had come by toil. This I had learned in my youth, when I was a farmhand.

"I used to read books myself . . . long ago." He wrinkled his forehead as if he were seeing himself when he was young. "But my father had no use for them. He said they were mouse-traps for fools. I had three books the teacher had given me for my own. He burned them one day when I was out in the fields. He said there was no decency in them."

"What were they?" I asked, wondering what books a village school teacher would have given a boy.

He did not answer, but said instead, "He was a great man. He stayed here three years and then went away. He was full of dreams about the world, and about Ireland, too. But such dreams come better when you sleep in Dublin-town than here in Kerry." He smiled and drank his stout. "The last year he was here, we acted a play. My father said that it made no sense."

"What became of him?" I asked. "Has he ever come back?"

"Five years ago. He's a big man now, but old. Works for the government . . . Came in a new car. Spoke nothing but Irish while he was here." My companion shook his head, as if there were some mystery to be found in that. "My father, too, spoke in the language of the old; he said it was better for cursing than the king's."

"And you, you speak Gaelic, too?"

"I do, when I plow and the blade hits a rock, I give it a word or two in the language that such stones might know. But to my father I always spoke English after I was grown, and he would answer me in the old tongue." He chuckled. It was a joke that had gone on for decades in some remote fields and only the two of them to savour it.

I glanced at the woman at the end of the bar. She had been listening to our every word; but now she looked away, as though she didn't care.

"Still, he was a decent man. He fought in the war."

I knew what he meant, for in Ireland there is only one war; and if that ever stops, what will happen then?

"He knew Michael Collins. He said they were friends." The farmer's lips were curved as if it gave him pleasure to doubt his father's words.

"Michael Collins had many friends," I said and he finished the sentence for me.

"And enough of the other kind to get himself killed."

While I agreed, I thought, 'If and when he votes, it is not out of conviction, but out of spite. Politics in this part of the country is a family affair; it has to do with love and hate, not economics or party platforms.' The rain was letting up. I caught a glimmer of blue sky through the window. I wanted to leave but it was my turn to treat. I called the woman and ordered a pint for my friend and mumbled something about having far to drive, as an excuse for not ordering one for myself.

"He was all made of pride." My companion's mind had returned to his father. "Pride you cannot bend, it can only break."

"And your mother?" I asked.

He shrugged his shoulders and said, "She died when I was too young to remember. It was himself that brought me up, as he told me often enough." Then, as if it suddenly had occurred to him, he pointed to the woman at the end of the counter, and remarked, "Her mother was my mother's sister. We are cousins, we two."

Again the woman interrupted our conversation as if she were part of it. "He stayed with us until he was five," she explained.

"And we slept in the same bed." The farmer grinned and winked at me.

"There was no sin in that, we were but children, both." The woman turned her head and looked at me. "He comes every Tuesday; then he climbs back up the mountain to sit and sulk . . . But there's no harm in him."

I looked at my man. It was true what she said, there was no harm in him. I expected him to get angry at her comment; but he looked more as if it had pleased him.

'They live so close together,' I thought, 'that each one knows the other's faults and virtues as well. No wonder that some of them run away to the city. On their lonely hillsides, under that great sky, there is no privacy to be had. He misses that father he hated; and he comes here to bathe in her contempt and her love, too. It is a miserable life, but the only one he knows.'

"I fought him once. It was long ago. I must have been twenty-four or twenty-five. It was about the hay. I said it could wait cutting a day or two, he said we were to start that morning." My companion turned his pint glass around and around on the counter and grinned shyly. "The hay didn't matter, either to him or to me. It was pride and we knew it, both of us. We fought in the yard in front of the house, but he was stronger and beat me until I cried." Something in his voice made me aware that he was proud of his father; and if he had had a son, he would have done the same to him.

"What does it matter now?" The woman said the words as if she had said them many times before.

He raised his head and met her gaze, then he nodded in agreement; this, too, I felt sure he had done often. "It wasn't his fault. I should have left . . . But I wanted to fight him again. I thought, if I could only wait a while." He lifted his glass and drank. "It was not wrong of him. He wanted to be himself on the farm, what else could a decent man do but fight?"

"And did you fight again?" I asked.

He shook his head. "We never did . . . Somehow it did not matter." He smiled at the woman behind the counter and she smiled back; and for a moment, I knew what she must have looked like when she was young.

'There is sweetness both in victory and defeat. He had been left with his grudge, and his father? God knows what he had derived out of that fight on that lonely farm . . . Maybe, we all have to fight our father — at least, to know that we are men,' I thought; but it gave me no pleasure. I like my arithmetic to be more complex than that.

Two men entered the bar. I guessed them to be farmers. They greeted my friend and the woman behind the counter with a familiar air. This was the moment for me to leave. We exchanged "God Blesses," and "Good lucks," and then I was outside in the open air again.

The mountains behind the town were shaggy and bald in patches, poor land. The town, itself, a dreary place; there were no rivers near for Dublin or Cork anglers or any sights of interest to make tourists stop. The houses were shabby, as if the inhabitants knew that there was no point in keeping up appearances. 'Yet they are all decent men and women,' I thought, as I paid my bill at the garage; and then with self-pity added, 'Who knows if it is any worse here than everywhere else.'

But as I sped out of town, I knew I was wrong. There are places in which it is a curse to be born. The mountain had taken the sunlight from that overgrown village, it was not a fit stage for either tragedy or comedy. "That is why they never fought again," I mumbled to myself. "There was no point in it, in that place."

JOHN GARDNER

Publish and Be Conned

The story — like all true tales kept safe within the confines of a particular profession — is now well-known to most of the publishing fraternity. They laugh about it, over lunches and during after-meeting chatter in Dublin, London and New York. But it is rarely repeated outside that compound which encloses the men and women who deal with books.

Even within the profession, there are those in front of whom it is not wise to mention the incident. Paul McGrath — of McGrath-O'Malley, Publishers, Dublin — is one. Another is Gerald Roper, Chairman of that hallowed firm, Hotchkiss & Firmin, the highly-respected house that has published so many great literary names in London, since Aaron Hotchkiss first established the business in 1851.

McGrath-O'Malley is, as everybody knows, a more recent venture compared to Hotchkiss & Firmin. They have a steady, if not vast, yearly turnover; and their list, nowadays, is realistic for the market — Irish poetry, some excellent guide books, first rate academic works on Irish architecture and history, plus the occasional luxury coffee table book (you will recall their great success with the large and glossy *Irish Cottage Industries* — with its fifty colour prints and one hundred and twenty line drawings — which sold like the proverbial hot cakes a couple of years ago).

It was a different tale, however, in the early 1960's, when Paul McGrath and Patrick O'Malley scraped together just enough capital to start their own business. Mind you, they were young then; and, possibly, more brash. Paul had spent six years in publishing world of London, and had his contacts — and ideas. Both men were ambitious. There was no doubt about that; and they were prepared to work all hours.

I suppose you might have called them high-flyers. Certainly they both declared they were about to set the world on fire, and show everybody that Irish publishing could compete on the world market. An admirable and attainable ambition.

For relatively small sums of money, they set about collecting authors, and quickly landed a pair of established Irish poets (who have since moved to America where they appear to be writing movie scripts); and three novelists who had started well, with reasonable sales through English publishers. As often happens, however, these three had, after initial modest success, dropped into the doldrums and were only too pleased to accept advances of around £200, signing contracts with McGrath-O'Malley, and promising a novel each within twelve months. There were other contracts as well, and the two young men did their sums, checked the answers, and looked forward to reasonable and profitable returns within the first two years.

That was until the advent of Jack Rourke.

If Paul McGrath could be persuaded to talk about the thing, today, he would have to admit that he allowed his enthusiasm to rule his actions. By all the known guidelines of his chosen trade and profession, he should have made some enquiries about Jack Rourke. But the very charm and humour of the man swept Paul along on a wave, from the top of which he thought the gilded palaces and golden domes of a great publishing coup could be clearly seen. In plain language, within two days of Jack Rourke walking into his office, Paul McGrath imagined that he had glimpsed a huge crock of gold at the end of Rourke's rainbow.

The rainbow in question was a manuscript. Five hundred pages of manuscript to be exact: neatly typed, not a word misspelled, not a dot or comma out of place. Even its title, *The World Forsakers* (obviously culled from Arthur O'Shaughnessy's *Ode: We are the Music Makers*) had an international literary smack to it.

Rourke himself assisted in the hard sell, before even a page was read. He bounced — big, bearded and slightly drunk — into Paul McGrath's office one Tuesday morning with the words, "I'm here to make our fortunes."

What ambitious young publisher could resist such a claim? In truth, most would fight it to the last tin of printer's ink. But, Paul McGrath was younger and more ambitious than most. Besides, his partner was away for a few days, scouring West Cork for an elderly novelist, who had been famous in his day and was now said to be holed up, living like a hermit, somewhere near Skibbereen.

So, Paul went off with Jack Rourke, leaving the thick manuscript on his desk, and the pair of them took some liquid refreshment in a bar off O'Connell Street, and, later, in another on the far reaches of Stephen's Green.

Naturally it was not until the next morning — and even then with a severe beating in his head, and eyes that looked like traffic lights stuck on Stop — that Paul McGrath actually opened Rourke's manuscript.

Within twenty pages he knew there was something to it. Within a hundred he was certain that it was more than just something. There was pure magic in the book. It had everything: strong characterisation; almost poetic descriptive passages which did not descend to the banal; and, best of all for the publisher searching for a huge best-seller, there was this strong, internationally-flavoured narrative.

There was no trace of sentiment; the hero was Irish-American, and the action moved between Russia at the time of the Revolution, to London, and then to Spain, on the brink of its Civil War. Its theme was of a modern man caught in the great and changing world events of that time: a man trying to identify with the altering social and political ideas and ideals of the centuries first three decades: a man lost and found.

Four days after Jack Rourke first appeared in his office, Paul McGrath offered him a contract — £2,000 (huge for their small firm): half down, and half on publication, with a half share of all subsidiary rights.

Hearty and charming though he was, Jack Rourke displayed a great shrewdness.

"No doubt you'll be approaching the English and the Americans?" he asked.

"No doubt. Almost immediately. Once you've put your name to it." McGrath kept pushing the pen into Rourke's hand, quivering in anticipation.

Rourke read through the contract again, then said he would sign it if an additional clause was inserted giving him immediate access to his shares of the subsidiary rights as they came in.

Paul McGrath agreed: though he, naturally, pointed out that the main targets — England and America — would probably only pay a third of the total monies on signature of any major contract.

He really should have been alerted by Jack Rourke's reply — for which I can personally vouch, for, at the time, I was, as they used to say, "walking out" with McGrath's secretary.

Jack Rourke mused for a few seconds and then said, "Well, you'll have to make certain you get one hell of a lot of money for it in London and New York, for I'm counting on my share of that first third being something to shout about."

But Paul was not alerted, thinking it the most natural thing in the world. Authors, particularly authors of first novels who may, or may not, realise they have genius in them, are always obsessed with getting their hands on as much loot as possible. It is a fallacy that great literary figures think only of their art and craft. Just as it is a bigger fallacy to imagine that publishers are in the business for literary prestige alone.

Rourke signed the contract. Paul McGrath paid over a cheque for £1,000, and Patrick O'Malley almost had a heart attack when he returned to Dublin — having found the old author, long buried, near Skibbereen.

O'Malley — unfortunately no longer with us, though his name lives on with the firm — ranted and raged at Paul McGrath for parting with £1,000 to an unknown author. But McGrath merely smiled. Wait, he told O'Malley — for the manuscript of *The World Forsakers* was being copied, and that would take a few days.

Patrick O'Malley waited, fuming, but his choler passed quickly once he read the work. "Not just a literary masterpiece," was his verdict, "but a book that will appeal to the masses." The implication being that 'the masses' have no real appreciation of literary merit, but would go for the blood and guts of the narrative. "Paul, we have found a new Irish genius," he said.

Paul McGrath did not argue. He smiled, knowing for sure that it was *he* who had found the genius.

Straining their finances to the limit, McGrath took off, first for London, and then New York.

His publishing contacts in London, having been in the business for a long time, were unimpressed by his enthusiasm. They promised to read the manuscript and smiled pleasantly. But Paul had picked up a few tricks. He knew just how long most British publishers took to read manuscripts — anything from two to six months, particularly if it is by an unknown author. There is a case for having a shrine for the unknown author, with an eternal flame and everything.

Paul played his trump card. He was off to New York, he said, and was giving copies of *The World Forsakers* to five major publishing houses in London. He would be in London for one week. This was the hottest property that would come their way this year — maybe this decade — so they had to make up their minds in double-quick time. There would be no second chances. He was, in effect, setting up an auction; and, in the early 1960s, the London publishing houses regarded auctions with grave suspicion.

Within two days, McGrath had one of the selected publishers on the telephone making a quick offer of £10,000 if he would throw in the paperback rights.

McGrath rejected it out of hand. In those days £10,000 was quite a lot of money for a book — it is still not peanuts — but the idea of throwing in the paperback rights tipped him off. The publisher concerned had, presumably, already done a deal with the paperback firm in the event of acquiring the book.

The upshot of the London trip was that Gerald Roper, of Hotchkiss & Firmin, finally offered £20,000 with half of the money down on signature — unheard of for a first novel at that time.

The facts of the deal made the gossip columns in a lot of English newspapers — the price quoted being inflated, of course, as it always is. The Irish newshawks were also soon on to it, and, by the nature of things, the bush telegraph crossed the Atlantic well ahead of Paul McGrath.

Joseph L. Buckingham — of Rapport Press, Fifth Avenue, New York, New York — got *The World Forsakers* for the handsome sum of $100,000, and McGrath drove a hard bargain. Half the money down, on signature — as with Hotchkiss & Firmin. The signatures were flourished, and money changed hands.

Incidentally, Joseph L. Buckingham is no longer with us. Nor is Rapport Press, Fifth Avenue, New York, New York. The latter was swallowed into a multi-national company, following the former succumbing to a surfeit of Cuba Libres while on the town with a well-known editor of an even better-known publishing combine, which, for the sake of this report, we shall call Treblenight & Co Inc.

Back in Dublin, McGrath-O'Malley's bank account looked

very healthy; as did Jack Rourke's account. Initially he had cleared some £15,000, before the book even went to press.

Paul McGrath regaled him, over steak and a great deal of liquor, with dreams of the prizes yet to come — paperback sales, film rights, foreign rights, serial rights. The whole mad carousel. But Rourke seemed most contented with his cut to date.

Plans now became well advanced. McGrath-O'Malley had the good sense to keep things in proportion. They still gave at least a third of their time to the rest of their list. But two-thirds went on *The World Forsakers.* Things moved apace in London and New York. Jack Rourke was scheduled to visit England and America on "National Promotion Campaigns". It really was the big time. Dates of publication were announced — simultaneous publications being thought the most effective measure — while paperback houses and movie companies did cartwheels trying to get their hands on the rights to the book.

McGrath would have gone ahead and done deals all over the place, had it not been for Roper and Buckingham who, old hands that they were, counselled him to hold back. "Wait until the hardback's off the ground," they echoed each other. "Then there'll be real money in it."

So, to ten days before publication, when the first hint of danger flared McGrath's nostrils. He telephoned Jack Rourke, who still continued to live in a somewhat seedy apartment house on the North side of Dublin. His telephone was, in fact, coin-operated and on a landing, serving several tenants. It was also often out of order.

To start with, Paul McGrath was not unduly concerned when he failed to get Rourke on the 'phone. But, after two days, he decided to visit their genius author personally. Time was pressing, and Jack Rourke would soon have to be off to London and New York.

He was still unworried as he approached the address. A few minutes later, however, McGrath's unconcern blossomed into anxiety; then into sheer panic. Jack Rourke, he was told, had "sold his bits and pieces last week; paid the rent, and gone." Gone where? Abroad, they said. Jack had told them he was off, pockets jingling. No forwarding address.

"First night nerves," proclaimed Patrick O'Malley. "The fella's got cold feet. Success can do that to a man." Nevertheless they felt obliged to not only put the Gárdaí on to finding Jack Rourke, but also a private detective agency which specialised in missing persons.

Needless to say, they did not mention the disappearance to either Gerald Roper, of Hotchkiss & Firmin, Publishers, London; or Joseph L. Buckingham of Rapport Press, New York, New York. Rourke would turn up. Rourke had to turn up. Rourke would be a fool if he did not turn up. But even if he did not, they had the book. Maybe Rourke would not turn up, and in that case all the beautiful money owed to him, when all the deals were in and royalty statements prepared, would collect a nice spot of interest for McGrath-O'Malley.

The real blow fell on Saturday.

It was Paul McGrath's practice to browse around the second-hand bookshops on a Saturday morning. He was sorting idly through a pile of old fiction in one such shop in Clare Street, when a dog-eared, cheaply-bound, item caught his eye.

He flicked open the first couple of pages, noting that it had been published in 1939 by a very prestigious London house. In fact it went through his mind that he really should have included this publisher on his list of five when he had first put *The World Forsakers* up for auction. The title of the book now in his hand was *A Dream at Pleasure,* and that struck a vague chord. He repeated it several times.

A Dream at Pleasure had been written by a woman, whose name was certainly unfamiliar to him. Then McGrath turned to page one, chapter one, and was nearly sick on the spot.

The trees hardly moved, he read, *but the sea, lying before him, was flecked and frosted with white plumes. A strange phenomenon.*

He read on, feeling more sick. He even felt dizzy.

Taking a few deep breaths, Paul McGrath stumbled to one of the assistants, purchasing *A Dream at Pleasure* for two shillings (they had not yet started to use Monopoly money in the early 1960s).

I should imagine that he will still find it difficult to remember how he got home with the book. Certainly, when he arrived there, he slumped into a chair and started to read.

Maybe, on his way back, McGrath realised that the title of this book — *A Dream at Pleasure* — also came from O'Shaughnessy. The same poem: *We are the Music Makers* — the famous *Ode*:

> *One man with a dream, at pleasure,*
> *Shall go forth and conquer a crown;*

By then he must have known the real answer, for, of course, the first lines of *A Dream at Pleasure* were identical with the first lines of Rourke's *The World Forsakers.*

It did not take him long to discover that — apart from all the characters' names being changed, and a few minor alterations — the book published in 1939 was, word for word, identical with the book that he was to publish (a world bestseller even before it hit the shops) in a week's time.

Paul McGrath had only one, final, desperate idea that might just save the day. He knew the Editor-in-Chief at the London publishing house through which *A Dream at Pleasure* had first seen the light of day in the late 1930s. Quickly, he checked all possible reference books and could find no mention of the lady who had written *A Dream at Pleasure.* Obviously the book had died the death — it would have done at that time, when the world was about to plunge itself into the madness of yet another war.

He did not wait until the Monday morning, but put a telephone call through to the Editor-in-Chief of the famous London publishing house, at his home number. When he finally got through, Paul McGrath tried to sound as calm as possible.

"Sorry to bother you over the week-end, Tom."

"Paul, not at all. Good to hear from you. Gather you're going to rake in millions with this new find of yours. They've been playing it very close to the chest here. I haven't even been able to lay my hands on a copy."

McGrath sighed with relief. Part of the promotion campaign had been a come-on of silence. Newspaper and magazine literary editors were supplied with one review copy each, but had been asked, specifically — as a favour — not to part with it, or pass it on until publication day. That had been Buckingham's idea. "Shroud it in mystery, son. Secrecy. Except with regard to money, of course."

Slowly, Paul came to the matter in hand. "Look, Tom. This is almost certainly stupid — long before your time. Just checking. I'm making enquiries about a book your house published back in 1939. Probably some estate owns the rights. I can't trace the author, but I'm interested in extracts, for a reprint job. Interesting material."

"Long before my time. Give me the title, though — and the author's name — and I'll chase up the records on Monday. If we've still got them."

Paul McGrath repeated the title, slowly, and there was a long pause at the other end of the line. A pause which lengthened into silence, and stretched into infinity.

At last the Editor-in-Chief spoke. "I suppose you know who really did write that book? You're having me on, Paul."

McGrath spluttered and stalled.

"Obviously you don't. Would you believe that *A Dream at Pleasure* was written by. . . ." he mentioned the name of one of the western world's foremost lady authors: a name so revered that some claim you should genuflect as you say it. "Her first work. . . ."

Paul McGrath felt sick again, hardly taking in what the man on the London end was saying.

"She published it under her real name. Absolute flop. Didn't do a thing. Not even one review. I think they sold about a hundred copies. Funny you should call, though. Suspicious even, Paul. She's been working on a complete rewrite over the last year. We're doing it in April: under the original title of course. Well, if you really didn't know, you show very good taste in books."

Hardly had McGrath replaced the telephone when it rang again. He had left both his office and home numbers with the Gárdaí and the detective agency. It was the agency that specialised in missing persons. "Your Jack Rourke," a disembodied voice began.

"Yes?"

"You've got a right lad there, Mr. McGrath. Jack Rourke is one of six aliases. He's not wanted at the moment as far as I can find out — except by you that is. It's usually the Gárdaí, or some police force that's after him. Money mostly: bouncing cheques, credit cards, minor fraud, that kind of thing."

"Good Lord." Paul tried to sound surprised. It was not hard.

"Served six months in England a couple of years back," the disembodied voice continued. "Simple fraud. Six months in Wormwood Scrubs. 'The Scrubs' as they call it over the water."

"Ah."

"What did you want him for, Mr. McGrath?"

"Oh, he sent us a book that's all."

The voice at the other end laughed. "Up his street, that," it said. "Jack Rourke — or Richards as he was calling himself then — did his six months in The Scrubs working in the library."

Well, that just about said it all. Naturally there was a huge cover-up. The wrath of the famous lady author would have been horrific: the legal costs unbearable.

Money did change hands — mainly from McGrath-O'Malley to Hotchkiss & Firmin and Rapport Press. Not all of it, because Jack Rourke already had his cut. A nice slice for a man like Rourke. Everybody lost but him. Now everybody chuckles at his nerve.

He was not heard of again. Not under that name. The three publishers certainly did not search for him. They felt there was enough folly in the world already without calling attention to their own — for they had all been taken.

A couple of years ago, though, I happened to be in Corfu. There was this bar I visited most nights. A big, bearded Irishman seemed to be part owner, and was always the best of company. He knew everybody, even the two week package tourists, within five minutes. He would call them all by their Christian names, and they called him Jack.

When he got very drunk, which was most nights, he would take to reciting O'Shaughnessy's *Ode: We are the Music Makers.*

I often wondered about him, and will always remember his voice, melodic, even in drink. Magical in a way, as he spoke the verse—

We are the music makers,
We are the dreamers of dreams,
Wandering by lone sea-breakers,
And sitting by desolate streams,
World-losers and world-forsakers,
On whom the pale moon gleams:

And later, particularly as he recited—

One man with a dream, at pleasure,
Shall go forth and conquer a crown;
And three with a new song's measure
Can trample a kingdom down.